THE CRIME BEAT

EPISODE 1: NEW YORK

A.C. FULLER

VIVID BOOKS

1

Sunday

THE OLD MAN'S life flashed through his mind as he methodically unpacked the rifle. His calloused hands had aged, but the muscle memory created by hundreds of repetitions still lived in his fingers. Laying the base of the weapon on his lap, he attached the barrel, locked the take-down pins into place, and affixed the scope. Finally, he rested the spiked feet on the soft tar at the edge of the townhouse roof.

His back ached. Sharp pulses of pain coursed through his right knee. But the pain was worth it. His shot would change the world.

Gritting his teeth, he dropped to his stomach and took in the crowd. Six stories down and across Fifth Avenue, a couple hundred people had gathered on the wide marble steps of the Metropolitan Museum of Art to greet the arrivals of celebrities and billionaires with *ooohs*, *aaahs*, and countless photos. This is what America has become, he thought. A handful of elites hoard the wealth and the sheeple snap pictures and praise them for it.

He scanned the crowd and whispered the twenty-nine words in a hoarse monotone. "An international brotherhood, united by General Ki for a singular mission: to end the great replacement, to restore the sovereignty of nations, to birth a new era of freedom." He'd repeated the words dozens of times each day for a year. Today he would do his part to put them into action.

A blur of faces met his eye through the rifle scope, but Raj Ambani's face wasn't one of them.

Staying cool in stressful situations is what makes a sniper a sniper. Fifty years back, he could make a kill shot in less than a second without noticing the bombs going off around him. *Floating in the zone*, he called it. His primal energies focused on the target, his vision like a laser, sound muted so he barely heard the crack of his weapon as he pulled the trigger. Just silence and a man going limp, dead before hitting the ground. Back in the shit, if a bomb or an errant batch of napalm was going to land on his head, it was better to be oblivious anyway. Better to lock in and make the kill.

At his peak, he could touch a man half a mile away. He'd trained on a Remington M40, a modified Remington 700—one of the most popular rifles among hunters and the weapon of choice of Vietnam-era snipers. But this rifle was a custom job, state of the art and heavier than the M40 due to the oversized suppressor. Its barrel was even coated with a polymer-ceramic protectant that prevented corrosion and wear over time. Not that it mattered. He would use this gun only once.

The late afternoon was cloudy and unseasonably warm for mid-December in New York City—between fifty and fifty-five degrees with no wind. His wrinkled hands were more prone to shake now, but the shot would be easy enough. No more than three hundred yards and at an angle that made him almost feel sorry for his target. *Almost.*

Eye in the scope, he moved from person to person. A pair of young girls aimed phones at the crowd. A fat man craned his neck for a better view. Reporters jostled for space before a velvet rope that protected a red carpet running up the center of the steps. A black limousine—its extra large wheel wells and sturdy tires suggested it was armored—stopped between the rope lines in front of the red carpet.

The man slowed his breathing as he lightly touched the trigger. It was all about control. Any elevation of his pulse could throw the shot. He'd taken metoprolol for his heart for years, experimenting with the dose until he'd found the perfect balance. The beta blockers would have disqualified him from competition shooting, but he wasn't here to collect trophies.

His index finger was sweaty inside the leather glove. Leather was hot and cumbersome, but prints could bleed through latex and cloth often left traceable fibers.

The hairs on the back of his neck tingled and the world around him fell silent as the limo door opened. With a long, slow exhale, he allowed most of the air to leave his chest. A tall brunette stepped out of the limo and waved to the crowd. The crowd cheered.

The old man inhaled. It was only some self-absorbed movie star, filming herself with a cellphone as she walked the red carpet. Not his target.

Moving his eye from the scope, he glanced up and down the street. A white SUV limousine turned onto Fifth

Avenue a block away. It slowed and stopped in front of the Met. He trained the scope on the license plate: @3COMMA.

That was it. The custom plate matched Raj Ambani's Twitter handle, and he'd had to look up the meaning. Two commas in your net worth meant you were a millionaire. Three meant you were a billionaire. It wasn't enough to brag about his wealth, Ambani had to promote his Twitter account in the process.

He exhaled, letting his chest sink into the roof, waiting for the rear door to open. Everything dropped away except for his eye in the scope and his finger on the trigger. All sound around him faded.

The rear door didn't open. Instead, a portly driver emerged and waddled around the limo. He opened the rear door, his wide back shielding Ambani as he got out.

The .50 BMG round could easily pass through the fat man and take out the target behind him. But that wasn't part of the plan. Too risky.

He could wait. It had been fifty years since his last kill. And at seventy-three years old, this would likely be his last.

He wanted to savor the moment.

Halfway up the steps, Raj Ambani turned to face the reporters who'd followed him from the limo. "This evening is *not* about me, but I'll take a few questions about IWPF. If they're not about the cause we're here to support, I'll head inside."

A young woman shoved an iPhone in his face, its screen displaying the wavy red lines of a recording app.

"The deal with X-Rev International? Is that going through?"

Ambani stuck his hands in the pockets of his tuxedo pants. He was thirty years old and slightly built, his black hair slicked back and parted in the center. One of his companies had developed an early version of the recording app the reporter was using, and, despite her annoying question, he had to smile at seeing his work in action. Plus, he was in his element, as comfortable with the press as he was in the boardroom. He turned his unflinching smile on her. "Thanks, Sophie, but—again—IWPF questions only. Please."

"I'm a business reporter," she countered. "I *have* to ask about the merger."

He'd done enough interviews to know he could ignore questions he didn't want to answer. "The IWPF is an organization I'm proud to support. I've teamed with donors from the financial and tech sectors to establish an international legal team dedicated to protecting the wildlife of all nations, and of our precious oceans. The fifty-million-dollar fund will allow IWPF to blaze a trail in international law, creating protections for animals in an increasingly global society. As our economies and production bases become more interdependent, so must our conservation efforts."

A stocky male reporter elbowed his way to the front. "Raj, if we promise to get our science editors to write about…" He glanced at his notes, "…IPWF…or whatever…will you comment on the X-Rev merger?"

Ambani frowned. "It's I, W, P, F. The International Wildlife Protection Fund. And no, not today."

Ignoring a torrent of shouted questions, Ambani stood motionless on the steps. He scanned the crowd for an environmental reporter to call on. His limo pulled away below, and he wished he was in it. No matter how much good he did with his wealth, reporters only cared about how he'd gotten it, and how he was trying to get more.

He raised both hands, silencing the reporters. "No more questions. It's a beautiful Sunday evening in Manhattan and we're about to give fifty million dollars to an important charity." His white-toothed grin widened. "Come bug me about X-Rev on Monday morning if you must. Inside there's a glass of champagne with my name on it."

The thought of champagne made him salivate. He allowed himself one glass per week, and tonight was the night. Ambani loved New York City around the holidays, and he looked over the crowd to take it in. Across the street, twinkling Christmas lights decorated a Red Maple in front of a beautiful old limestone townhouse. A pair of pigeons emerged from the tree and flew south. He breathed in the cool air, which carried a sweet-smokey scent from a nearby roasted nut cart. Life was far from perfect, but it was beautiful.

As the birds disappeared into the evening, an unexpected movement pulled his gaze to the roof of the townhouse. A second twitch of motion focused his attention on what appeared to be a man with a black rifle.

As he watched Ambani watch the birds, the old man whispered. "An international brotherhood, united by General Ki to carry out a singular mission: to bring an end to the great replacement..." Ambani looked up at the roof just as he reached the end of the words. "...to restore the sovereignty of nations, to birth a new era of freedom."

His forehead was like a target. Wide and brown against the backdrop of cream-colored marble. The world dropped away. Everything except the target, his right index finger, and the words. He let his breath out slowly. He grew still. He was floating in the zone. Ready to kill.

Ambani's eyes widened as he saw him, but it was too late.

The man pulled the trigger once. A hissing *pop* came from the gun.

His target went slack before anyone heard the shot. The round could penetrate a truck engine at close range. His shot had entered clean, piercing Ambani's forehead and turning his brain to jello on the way out, leaving a fine, red-mist plume. He never knew what hit him.

Before the body hit the ground, the man was taking the gun apart.

Shrieks filled the air as his senses returned to him, but the words moved through his mind, drowning them out.

A minute later, he slung the rifle bag over his shoulder and hobbled toward the ladder on the back of the townhouse. For the first time, his wrinkled face broke out in a wide grin. He'd done his part. The small part he'd been called on to perform. The small part in a worldwide pact that would usher in a new age of freedom.

2

JANE COLE WAS PISSED. She'd been pissed at the world for three years, but right now her boss was catching the brunt of it.

She slammed a fist on his desk, rattling a jar of pens and knocking a wire-bound reporter's notebook off the table. She regretted it immediately, but was burning too hot to apologize. "The weeks before Christmas are especially tough."

Max Herr grabbed his notebook from the floor, then kicked his feet up on the desk, lacing his hands through his thick white hair. "No problem. I get that you're passionate about this issue. We're *on* the same side here."

She needed this job, and the two vanilla lattes she'd chugged before the meeting were doing nothing to calm her. From anger, she had only one place to go. With the flick of an internal switch, she sighed and her anger morphed into numbness. Her thoughts became white noise—static with a frequency between the crackling of a radio and the gentle whoosh of the cosmic noise app she used (with half an Ambien) to fall asleep each night. She flicked this switch a few dozen times a day. It kept her sane.

Max squinted. "Jane, are you okay? The story was good, but I'm catching hell for it. I know you're passionate about this, but—"

She shot out of her chair. "You're not?" The static was gone. The numbness disappeared. The anger was back.

Herr held up his hands. "I've greenlit more stories on police brutality than any editor in the city, but I'm more passionate about *accuracy*."

"My story *was* accurate. Every word of it. Robert Warren smashed a suspect's face into the metal grate of his cruiser. That. Is. Fact." She shook her head and flopped into the chair. "Didn't you tell me when I started here that every negative story I wrote about the department would get pushback?"

Herr stroked his bushy white beard, nodding. "I'm getting more than the usual pushback. Warren called twice today, three times yesterday. His name was on the list for detective. He can kiss that goodbye."

"*Good!*" Jane snapped. "Brutal cops shouldn't get promotions."

Herr shook his head. "No, they shouldn't."

Going emotionally numb gave her power. The static darkness erased the pain but left her perceptive, allowed her to see others clearly. His terse answer made her wonder whether he truly agreed with her. She could read most people within three minutes. But she'd never been able to read her boss. He didn't look at the floor when he spoke. He never raised his voice when he lied. He had no discernible tell. His affable smile and white hair and beard reminded her of a kindly old wizard from the movies. It was a face that allowed everyone to believe he was on their side. In truth, the only side he was ever on was that of *The New York Sun*, the newspaper he'd run for the last ten years.

Since she couldn't read him, she kept pressing. "Max, he *smashed* a dude's face after arresting him. What more do we need to know?"

"All I'm asking is that you flip over some rocks to see what crawls out. I'm sure you got the facts right, but sometimes the facts are different than the truth. Got it?"

Cole relented. "Just because Warren calls three times a day doesn't mean he's innocent."

"Not only Warren. I've gotten calls from two others I trust. They say Warren is one of the good guys."

She waved a hand at him. "Cops protect their own. Always have. Especially against journalists."

Herr sighed. "You know I *am* still your boss, Jane."

"For now." She stopped halfway to the door of his office. "I remember when I could actually *hear* and *smell* the person I was reporting on. Now?" She waved her phone at him. "I'm a damn stenographer. I copy Twitter statements and hope someone calls me back. We break one story based on actual sources and the entire department comes after us. Makes a woman wonder whether there's any room to be a real reporter. I just don't think there's a point anymore."

Herr looked concerned. "A point to what?"

Through the windows of Herr's office, Cole gestured at the expansive newsroom, where a few dozen reporters, interns, and tech people typed at laptops, scrolled on phones, or talked quietly. "This. Any of it. *Anything*."

"I worry when you say things like that." He shook his head. "That and things like the little 'For now' comment you snuck in a moment ago. You survived four rounds of layoffs because you're brilliant and you write well. You're the only woman leading a crime beat at a major New York City paper. I know the last few years have been…"

She frowned at him and he smiled sadly.

"…Difficult isn't strong enough. I know it's been devastating. I mean, I can't know what you've had to go through. But you *made* it. You're still here."

"Nice pep talk, coach. I need to get back to my desk. My spidey sense tells me a police spokesman might be sending a tweet." She stopped in the doorway and swiveled to face him, but his eyes were on his laptop. "I'm gonna need to be ready to transcribe it *right away, sir*."

"Wait!" he called without looking up, his voice urgent. "Something at the Met. A shooting."

"Who?"

"It's Twitter so I'm not sure it's true. They're saying… oh, dear God… they're saying Raj Ambani was killed at a charity event at the Met."

Herr stood abruptly and waved for her to get out.

Cole met his eyes. "I'm sorry for…for all the…you're right, I'm still here. Christmas is just hard for me, okay?"

"Go! And call me the second you have something."

3

THE METROPOLITAN MUSEUM of Art spans four city blocks on the east side of New York City's Central Park. Bordering two police precincts—the Upper East Side's 19th and the special Central Park precinct—the famous museum is one of the crown jewels of Manhattan's Fifth Avenue.

Cole guessed that officers from the 19th would respond first. After evacuating the Met and securing the crime scene, they'd close the 79th Street Transverse, the road through Central Park that connects the east and west sides of Manhattan. So when she'd told the Uber driver to go farther north and cross the park at 84th, she was betting that the more northern crossing would still be open. She'd bet right. As she slid out of the car, two officers were setting up a barricade to block off the road.

"Turn around!" one of them shouted at the driver, waving his arms. "No more cars through here."

The driver pulled a u-turn as Cole approached the cop —an acne-scarred twenty-something Cole figured she could work. Most of the young ones weren't yet jaded

against reporters, not having had time to develop the
every-one-of-them-is-an-asshole-until-proven-otherwise
mindset so common to veteran cops. "The 79th Street
crossing was closed, too. What's going on?"

"Police business, ma'am."

The other officer was older and, Cole assumed, a little
wiser. He pulled another barricade off the police truck.
"Move along, lady."

She didn't recognize either of them. Grunts from the
19th, most likely. But they might have information. Her
competitors—mostly cute twenty somethings with huge
social media followings—would blow right past these two
and not think twice. But low-level cops were often willing
to talk.

On the ride from the office Cole had learned everything
she could about the shooting, which wasn't much. A
handful of blurry pictures had appeared on Twitter, along
with rumors about Ambani's murder, but nothing credible.
So far, the police had released no official statements. No
video of the shooting or its immediate aftermath had
emerged—a surprise since multiple TV crews had been
covering the event, and every person in Manhattan carried
a digital video camera in their pocket.

She made eye contact with the acne-scarred cop who'd
returned to the barricades—large blue sawhorses
connected by blue 2x4s and stenciled in white lettering
that read NYPD. "I'm Jane Cole from *The New York Sun.*
Mind if I ask you a couple questions?"

He stepped toward her aggressively, his face turning
cold. "Cole, huh? You wrote the hit job on Warren."

She stepped back. "I reported a brutal attack against a
suspect who had already been apprehended, yes."

His smile wasn't friendly. "Then, no. No you *can't* ask

us any questions. And not only that." He took out his phone and waved it in her face. "I'm gonna text every reporter at the *Times*, the *Post*, and the *Daily News* to give *them* a heads up on Ambani. Our precinct captain will sit for an hour on the record with the damn NYU student newspaper just to make sure you fall behind." He spat at her feet. "Rob's one of the best. That story made New York less safe." He turned and muttered, "Stupid bitch."

Cole grimaced and walked away. The animosity was nothing new, and she let it disappear into the void as she crossed the street. The Fifth Avenue sidewalk was blocked by police barriers, so she walked east, circled around on Madison, and approached the Met from 83rd, scanning every face she saw. A block ahead, three blue and white police vans were parked sideways across the traffic lane. A large crowd had formed. Necks craned to peek between the vans and a few dozen onlookers sat on people's shoulders, trying to peer over them.

"The shooter was on the roof," a man said as Cole passed.

He had wavy salt and pepper hair and wore a tan wool coat over a custom-tailored shirt. He'd been speaking with a woman who also looked rich. *Local residents.* "Where'd you hear that?" Cole asked casually.

"Didn't *hear* it." The man's haughty voice matched his outfit. "I know it. I live up there." He pointed to the top of a townhouse on the corner of Fifth Avenue and 83rd. "Furnace was stuck on high again, so I had my window open. Heard the shot, looked out...crowd was already scattering." He pointed to the steps of The Met. "I ran down, but it was too late. I'm a surgeon—not trauma, but still..." He studied the ground. "Never seen a head so...damaged. What was left of it." The doctor raised his head to meet her eyes again. "Anyway, by the time I tried to get back to my apartment, the whole area was on lockdown. Cops said the shots could have come from my building, but I'm pretty sure they came from next door." He pointed up again, this time to the limestone townhouse next to his.

Cole studied him. He had shallow lines around his eyes and an even tan. His face was stiff, but earnest. A rich guy, guilty about his wealth, who needed everyone to believe he was an honest, good person. The kind of guy who staved off the darkness by remaining above reproach at all times. He wasn't lying.

The fact that he was telling the truth didn't mean he was right, but it was a good start. She nodded at the townhouse. "That one?"

"Pretty sure."

"What did it sound like?"

"Kind of a shallow pop, not a huge bang."

The townhouse was five stories of old limestone that had recently been resurfaced. Typical Upper East Side home for millionaires or billionaires, though nicer than average due to the prime location. It was a townhouse that would cost eight to ten million dollars on a side street, but was probably worth double that because of the Fifth Avenue address.

She reached into her small hip purse—which her colleagues derisively called a "fanny pack"—and retrieved a business card. She held it out confidently. "Jane Cole, *New York Sun*. Okay if I follow up with you about this?"

The man frowned—a common response when people learned she was a reporter—but he took the card and pulled out one of his own.

"Dr. Martin Horowitz?" she asked, reading it. "The heart guy?"

"I'm *a* heart guy."

The woman next to him tugged at his sleeve playfully. "You know what she means, dear. You're *the* heart guy. On the East Coast, at least."

Cole stowed the card in the pocket of her black slacks. "Didn't you do the mayor's triple bypass?"

The doctor smiled proudly. "I did."

The woman next to the surgeon beamed. "He does *all* the important people because he's the best." The woman tilted her head and leaned in toward Cole. "But he works on *poor* people, too. Pro bono." Her lips curled slightly at the mention of 'poor people.' Cole crossed her arms. The work may have been pro bono, but it was all about projecting an *image* of compassion. Again, the need to be seen as good. "I'm Mrs. Horowitz, by the way, pleased to meet you. Martin and I are big fans of—"

"Thank you." She deflected the handshake and cut her off. "I'll follow up on that info."

An officer she vaguely recognized was making his way from the steps of The Met back to the police van barricade. She'd met him at Shooter's, but his name escaped her. Kenny? Or maybe...Remy?

Too bad she'd been three shots into a bottle of tequila when she'd met him.

4

SHE JOGGED up to him as he passed between two police vans. "Reggie?" she called, making her best guess. He turned, one eyebrow raised, but didn't say anything. "Jane Cole. From Shooter's. Remember me? The other night?"

He waved off another officer and gestured for Cole to follow him around the side of the van. "It's Benny, and yes, I remember. Patrón neat, right?"

"That's right."

"I shouldn't be talking with you."

"You look good in your uniform." She wasn't lying. He was about ten years younger than her, with a clean-shaven babyface that belonged on a boyband poster.

"Thanks, but you were at Shooter's with Danny, right?"

She flashed him a warm smile. "It's casual between Danny and me." She wasn't proud of using flirtation as a reporting technique, but most men were stupid enough to fall for it. And when she was after a story, she didn't leave anything off the table.

Benny narrowed his eyes, then smiled back. "C'mon, you're just working me for a story."

"About me and Danny—ask him yourself." She kept her smile as bright as a headlight high-beam for another second before letting it fade. "But you're right. I *am* working you for a story. I don't need you, though. I already know where the shot came from." She pointed at the roof of the townhouse. "Are you reviewing the building's security cameras?"

"Surrounding buildings, too." Benny stepped away. "But I really shouldn't be talking to you about it."

"I've been around crime scenes, Benny. I'm not asking for state secrets here. Of course you're checking video." She pulled out her phone and pretended to read from the screen. "Twitter says the shooting was racially motivated." She looked back at Benny but kept the look on her face open, as though it was an innocent question and not a technique to pry a crumb of information from the guarded officer. "Any comment?"

Benny reached for the phone, but Cole pulled it away. She didn't like lying—she wasn't very good at it—but sometimes that's what it took to get people talking.

He sighed. "Who the hell would say that? We don't even have a suspect yet and—"

"A hundred people on the steps when Ambani's head burst like a balloon and *no one* saw anything? C'mon, Benny, don't piss me off today."

"Ramirez!" An angry voice boomed from twenty yards away. "What the hell you talking to *her* for?"

Benny smiled. "See what you did? Now I'm in trouble." He leaned in close, too close, and inhaled deeply, like he was smelling her hair. "You owe me now. What are you doing tonight? Buy you a shot at Shooter's?"

Cole recoiled internally, but flashed a smile he was too dumb to know was phony. "I don't date sources."

"I'm not a—"

"Yes, you are," she called over her shoulder as she walked away.

On her way back through the crowd, she began composing her story in her head, but a series of shouts half a block south interrupted her.

"Get outta here!"

"Screw you!"

She hurried in the direction of the argument and found a lanky officer, arms folded stubbornly to serve as a barrier to another tall, well-built man, who seemed determined to get past the police barricades. The more solidly built man wore plain clothes, but his bearing suggested he, too, was an officer. He stood taller than six feet and his back and shoulder muscles filled out his blue button-down.

She sidled toward them, careful not to get too close, listening but not looking at them.

"You're not supposed to be here," the lanky officer said. "You *know* that."

"I can help." His voice was deep, and something about it was familiar.

"Then call the Captain. You know he has your back."

"And *you* know he can't take my calls."

"We *all* have your back, Rob, but until this thing plays out…"

Cole stopped in her tracks. *Rob?*

She held her phone over her head, pretending to look for a signal. From the corner of her eye, she glanced in the direction of the two men. The man in plainclothes had a thick, muscular neck and a gleaming bald head the color of onyx.

It was Robert Warren.

The man whose career she'd destroyed.

5

THE OLD MAN breathed in the greasy, fish-fried air as he slid the barrel of the rifle into the dumpster. Checking the alley one last time, he placed the gloves into a garbage bag full of fish skeletons, then mashed the bag down over the gun barrel. Tomorrow was trash day, so the final pieces of the weapon and the gloves would be in New Jersey by eight in the morning.

He hadn't touched the ammo or components of the weapon with anything other than leather gloves. Killers had been convicted by one strand of fiber, by a speck of clay on their boots matched to a scene by a unique chemical or molecular fingerprint. Every perpetrator brings in and takes out trace evidence at the scene. The less you leave behind, the better your chances of not getting caught.

Exiting the alley, he shot a look through the window of Trần's Fried Fish. He smiled at Duc, the owner, who waved for him to come in. He could go for an order of his lemongrass-fried cod right about now, but he didn't have the time. He'd spent the last hour stashing pieces of the weapon in storm drains and dumpsters across the Lower East Side. Now he needed to post the message.

He unlocked the faded red door of his apartment building and climbed three floors to his studio, one of two on the top floor of the narrow brick building. He examined the piece of hair he'd stuck to the doorknob plate with his own saliva. Had it been missing, he'd have known someone had been inside, or *was* inside waiting for him now.

Closing the door behind him quietly, he scanned the apartment. At a metal desk in the corner, he opened a black laptop and checked the security camera log. No activity had been registered since he left that morning.

It was silly, but a twinge of something, an insecure feeling, made him check the four corners of the room. Even though he had the physical and digital proof that no one had been in his apartment, he didn't completely trust the technology. Each camera stood guard in its place in the corner, resting on a brace and peering down to capture any movement.

He crossed the floor and opened the lone window. Outside, a rusty metal fire escape led down to the alley behind Trân's. The smell of fried fish wafted in, stirring his belly.

He walked to the kitchenette, a small space enclosed by a sliding wooden door. At the movement of the door, Jefferson looked up. He had the face and body of a bulldog and the black-and-white spots of a dalmatian. The man unhooked the chain that bound him close to the stove. "Jefferson, it's all over. Don't worry. We got him."

The dog, too weak to stand, set his head back on the floor.

"I'm sorry, Jefferson." He opened the refrigerator and

pulled out a pack of bologna, then slapped a piece on the floor in front of the dog. "Eat up, boy. It's over now. No more closet for you."

Jefferson didn't move.

"Eat the bologna."

Jefferson's eyes moved to the man's angry face, but his chin didn't lift from the floor. His energy was low, his eyes tired.

"Eat it!" He grabbed the bologna from the floor and pressed it into the dog's mouth.

Jefferson chewed it a few times half-heartedly, then spat it out.

"Stupid dog. I should have named you *Hamilton*."

He limped back to the desk, shoving slices of bologna in his mouth as he sat. Opening the anonymous Tor browser through his personal VPN, he navigated to DogLoverSupplies.Com, one of the many websites he and his brothers used. The NSA, CIA, and other government agencies monitored dark web chat rooms. Hiding their conversations deep in run-of-the-mill websites gave them several more layers of protection. Not that he was too worried about federal law enforcement or military intelligence. Most of the agencies who'd be after them were incompetent anyway. They'd lost Bin Laden for nearly ten years before finding him by random chance, hiding in plain sight. He'd often joked that the motto of U.S. intelligence and federal law enforcement should be "better lucky than good."

He navigated to the chat room buried deep in the backend of the site, where his brothers would be waiting. Undoubtedly, they'd already heard the news, but protocol required that he share it formally. The chat room was a simple black box with a blinking cursor. As he typed, his words appeared in plain white text on the screen.

T-Paine:

1/9

(NBC's Hero)

X

An international brotherhood, united by General Ki to carry out a singular mission: to bring an end to the great replacement, to restore the sovereignty of nations, to birth a new era of freedom.

1/9

(NBC's Hero)

X

He pressed "Enter" and waited, mashing the bologna around in his mouth. The expected response came a minute later.

Kokutai-Goji:

2/9

(The Silver Squirrel)

Initiated.

An international brotherhood, united by General Ki to carry out a singular mission: to bring an end to the great replacement, to restore the sovereignty of nations, to birth a new era of freedom.

2/9

(The Silver Squirrel)

Initiated.

The formalities over, congratulatory responses flooded in.

Gunner_Vision: *Saw it on the "news." Way to go, my U.S. brother.*

Tread_on_This!: *Step one, man, step one.*

He leaned back, lacing his hands together through his

thin, greasy hair. For the first time since the war, he was a success. He was a contributor—an actor, not a spectator. "C'mere, Jefferson. Come celebrate your daddy. We did a big thing today, buddy. Come love him. Come on, boy." The dog opened its eyes, but didn't move.

The old man looked at the screen, where a dozen new messages had appeared.

It's_Our_Country: *Cheers from across the pond. BBC running with the story.*

8/15/47: *Had it coming. His parents were deserters.*

As he read the messages, he stood and took an old wooden baseball bat out of a glass case on the wall above his computer. Signed by Roger Maris, he'd received it from the player himself during his record-setting 1961 season. Despite the pain in his back, he swung the bat, mimicking Maris's beautiful left-handed swing as best he could.

He felt a stirring in his chest, a feeling he hadn't known since he was a boy staring out at the green grass of Yankee Stadium. It was as though a wide open space had opened inside him, a space large enough to fit any possibility.

Freedom_2019: *It's happening.*

End_the_Great_Replacement: *They will know your name.*

He'd done it. Years of frustration had inspired months of planning, and now he'd done it. The world would one day celebrate him. More importantly, the world would celebrate this day as a new Independence Day.

For the first time since he could remember, he was free.

6

At the sight of Robert Warren, Cole shielded her face with her hand.

A college baseball player turned Marine turned cop, Warren wasn't just a big man, he was a specimen. She'd watched videos of his intense workout routines on Instagram while writing the story about him. Boxing. Weights. Running up hills in the park carrying a log over his wide shoulders. He may have been a brutal cop, but there was no denying that he took care of his body.

It wasn't his size that worried her, though. It was his temper. And, on top of that, the fact that he had more reason to hate her than anyone else in the city. She'd written stories about controversial police incidents before, usually stories of white cops roughing up minority suspects. The story on Robert Warren was her first involving a black cop and a white suspect. Not that it mattered. To her, a brutal cop was a brutal cop. And every time she'd written one, the subject had been furious.

She peeked around her hand to get a better look, and the officer noticed. Warren turned. If he recognized her, she'd be able to read it in his eyes. He didn't, and she tried to slip into the crowd.

"That's her. Rob, that's her." The voice of the lanky officer. His tone had shifted from confrontational to conspiratorial.

"Who?" Warren asked.

She didn't want this confrontation, but it was unavoidable, so she changed tack and took it head on. Swiveling on the heels of her leather flats, she strode forward and stuck out her hand. "My name is Jane Cole of the *New York Sun*. I'm the woman who ruined your life."

Warren took a deep breath and let it out slowly. Clearly, he was trying to keep his anger from overcoming him. It was interesting to see someone else's technique. When Jane herself needed to control the demon of anger, she went numb and lived in the static. Allowed pieces of herself to disappear into the background. Warren's technique made him more dominant. He seemed to grow somehow larger—as if that were possible—until he filled out more of his already huge frame.

"Jane Cole?" His voice was deep and steady. "The one who wrote the article?"

"The same one you've been threatening."

"Threatening the paper, with libel. I wasn't threatening *you* personally. If I threatened *you*, you'd know it." He turned to the lanky officer and sighed. "Anything worse than reporters?"

"Criminals?" the officer offered.

Warren scoffed. "Ask me, *she's* the real criminal."

Jane stood half a foot shorter than Warren and was probably half his weight. And though he was on paid leave, he was still a cop. Not the kind of guy she had any business threatening. The harsh light of a streetlamp shone down on her. She wanted to feel its light warming her, giving her courage, but the sun had set and a cold wind blew down Fifth Avenue. At times like this, the numbness served her work. Her life, his life, none of it mattered anyway. "Mr. Warren. *Rob*." She slid right in front of him and glared into his dark eyes. "You're a brutal cop and should be behind bars. I have your ex-wife's number. Call my office again, I'll get every reporter in the city to write about the period of your life after you left the Marines and before the department dropped its standards low enough to let a scumbag like you in. And to be clear"—she narrowed her eyes—"*that* was a threat."

His face twitched. His right hand clenched at his side. She felt his desire to punch her as a palpable presence in the air. Inside, she was a field of gray static that knew only one thing: she'd gotten the story right. This was just another knuckle-dragger with a badge and a gun.

Warren opened his mouth to speak, but she walked away before he could.

Half a block away, the adrenaline wore off. *What the hell had she just done?* She glanced back at Warren, hoping he hadn't pursued her. He stood there, arms crossed, staring right at her. He'd been watching her walk away.

To her shock, his face broke out in a wide grin.

7

AFTER STRIKING out with half a dozen cops and potential witnesses, Cole took a seat on the steps of a brownstone that sat on the edge of the crime scene. Twitter had nothing new on Ambani. Though his name was already trending worldwide—more than 800,000 tweets had been sent in the two hours since he died—nothing reliable was out there. Nothing story-worthy. On the ride from the office, she'd messaged a few of her best sources. No one had responded.

A sad irony struck her. Ambani's blood was freeze-drying on the marble steps no more than a hundred yards away. Dozens of cops, detectives, and FBI agents surrounded her. And there she was, sitting on a cold stone step, staring at her *phone* for information and messaging cops through their anonymous burner accounts. This was the crime beat, 2018.

She decided to look into Raj Ambani himself, hoping some detail from his life might lead to a good source outside the department. His Wikipedia page had already been updated with news of his death. Information travels fast. She kept reading.

Raj Ambani was the sixty-third richest man in the world, valued at $17.1 billion, according to Forbes. One of only a handful of American success stories on the list, Ambani's parents had immigrated from southern India in the mid 1980s, his father driving a taxi and his mother waitressing at Bombay Palace, a well-reviewed restaurant in the West Village.

From the time he was two, his parents knew he was special. Before he could speak in complete sentences, he could do multiplication and division. By the time he entered grade school, he was enrolled in a calculus class at City College. A 1994 newspaper article showed a six-year-old Raj, encircled by college freshmen, a pencil behind his ear and a serious look on his face. The opening line read, "His classmates call him 'Rain Man,' but Raj Ambani's parents believe he's the reincarnation of Srinivasa Ramanujan, the famous Indian mathematics prodigy of the early twentieth century."

When he was thirteen, Ambani received a full scholarship to Columbia University, where he graduated in three years with degrees in math and computer science. From there, he pioneered computer-based stock trading, using algorithms to predict stock movements in real time. His invention lessened the importance of human evaluations and recommendations in the stock market, ushering in an era of markets ruled by computers. He became a billionaire on his twentieth birthday. Most impressive to Cole was that he seemed to have made a smooth transition into adulthood. Two years ago, at twenty-eight, he'd married an opera singer who was expecting their first child any day.

"You've got guts."

Cole looked up from her phone. Rob Warren stood before her, hands in the pockets of his gray jeans.

"I respect guts, but I meant what I said about journalists being the lowest. If the facts won't sell papers, just make something up, right?"

She stood and climbed two steps to meet his eye level. "Lower than cops who abuse their power?"

"I *didn't* abuse—"

"Sure." She smiled sardonically.

"You don't know anything about me." He pressed his hands into his cheeks and blew out a long stream of air. He looked ready to explode.

"I know you beat up unarmed suspects. Or that you did, once. I know you want to hit me. I understand. Really. This world gives us plenty to be enraged about. Have you checked your blood pressure lately?"

Warren shoved his hands in his pockets, chuckling. "It's not good."

"And you thought getting in my face would help?"

Warren stepped back. "You don't know as much as you think."

"Let's not do this cops versus reporters thing, okay? It's a cliché."

Warren paced a little square. Two steps right, two steps forward, two steps left, two steps back. Military precision.

"Why did you come up to me?" Cole asked.

"I wanted to explain."

"Explain why you broke the nose of a prisoner? An unarmed man? A man innocent until proven guilty?"

Warren waved the air as though shooing a fly. "I mean the period after I got back from Afghanistan. You dangled it in front of me back there, threatened me, but that wasn't in your story. Why not?"

"Wasn't relevant to the story." It was a lie, but the real reason would weaken her position.

Warren scoffed. "That's a lie."

Now *he'd* read *her*. "Honestly, what you did after you got back from Afghanistan was your business. I never would have put that in a story."

"I appreciate that." Warren walked another square, alternating between deep breaths and the double face-palm that seemed to be his pressure release valve.

She sensed there was something else on his mind. "You wanna tell me the real reason you approached me?"

He returned to his original spot. "I want to tell you what I know about Raj Ambani."

8

THEY WALKED EAST for two blocks, Cole a dozen paces behind Warren and on the opposite side of the street. He'd lost the lower half of his right leg in Afghanistan, and now walked with an almost imperceptible limp.

When he'd approached her, information about Raj Ambani was the last thing she'd expected. In fact, Warren himself had seemed surprised by his words. A second after uttering the name, he'd whispered, "Meet me at the Star-bucks on east 87th in ten." Then he'd walked away.

Cole lifted the collar of her sleek blue coat against the cold wind as Warren turned north. When he passed under streetlights, she tried to make eye contact, but he marched forward, stone-faced, not looking back once.

Her piece on Warren hadn't been a hit job. It hadn't even been a big deal. Just another story about an NYPD cop abusing his power and the predictable department cover-up. The initial scoop had come from a direct message on

Twitter. It was her least favorite social media platform but the one that, increasingly, comprised a major part of her job. On a Monday night two weeks ago she'd picked up a follow from a user with no profile picture and only a half dozen followers. The user's handle was @NYPD_Watcher_NYPD and the bio read, "I tell the truth about cops."

Cole had followed back and, minutes later, received a direct message.

@NYPD_Watcher_NYPD: *I have information about an officer breaking a suspect's nose. Interested?*

@Cole_Jane_NewYorkSun: *Yes.*

@NYPD_Watcher_NYPD: *I could give this to anyone.*

@Cole_Jane_NewYorkSun: *But you chose me. Why?*

@NYPD_Watcher_NYPD: *You'll get it out fast, right?*

@Cole_Jane_NewYorkSun: *If it's what you say, you have proof, and I can verify it, yes.*

A minute went by before the next message, which contained a three-page PDF file. Cole read the document, an internal report on the incident. According to the report, at least one witness saw Robert Warren park his cruiser, open a rear passenger door, and smash a suspect's face into the grate that separated the back seat from the front. Dashcam video confirmed this.

@Cole_Jane_NewYorkSun: *Are you in the 30th?*

@NYPD_Watcher_NYPD: *No.*

@Cole_Jane_NewYorkSun: *IAB?*

@NYPD_Watcher_NYPD: *Ding ding ding. Boss is slow-rolling it.*

@Cole_Jane_NewYorkSun: *So, why me?*

@NYPD_Watcher_NYPD: *I tried The Times. They've had it two days.*

@Cole_Jane_NewYorkSun: *And?*

@NYPD_Watcher_NYPD: *Crickets.*

@Cole_Jane_NewYorkSun: *Why?*

@NYPD_Watcher_NYPD: *Dunno. Maybe they don't want to implicate a black cop?*

Just to be sure, Cole pulled up the metro section of *The New York Times* online. No mention of the incident.

@Cole_Jane_NewYorkSun: *I have to ask: you willing to go on record?*

@NYPD_Watcher_NYPD: *LOL.*

@Cole_Jane_NewYorkSun: *They'll confirm this is authentic?*

@NYPD_Watcher_NYPD: *They'll have to. The pain of a story like this coming out is less than the pain of denying it officially, then seeing it on page 1.*

Four hours later, Cole filed the story, complete with a denial from Robert Warren and a quote from a source in the 6th Precinct, admitting the troubling incident had occurred and assuring the good people of New York City that they would get to the bottom of it. *The Sun* ran the story on A1 of the print edition the next morning and on the homepage of the web edition. By noon, Warren had been suspended pending an investigation.

As she entered the Starbucks, Warren stood at the counter, ordering a double espresso. She paid for his coffee, plus a vanilla latte for herself, then followed him to the back. He picked a table in the corner and sat facing the wall—the least visible spot in the place.

Cole sipped her latte and raised an eyebrow at him. She'd let Warren do the talking. There was a chance he was trying to set her up, to discredit and embarrass her by planting a false story. Payback. Wouldn't be the first time a cop had tried it. But something in his demeanor told her he was for real.

Every few seconds he glanced over his shoulder at the door. The ceramic espresso cup almost disappeared in his large hands as he passed it back and forth nervously. "I shouldn't have come here."

"I can tell there's something you want off your chest."

He shot the espresso in one gulp, then pointed at her paper cup. "Sugar. Lot of sugar in a vanilla latte. Between the milk and the syrup, I'm guessing thirty to forty grams?"

Not what she'd expected. "How the hell would I know? Are you here to scrutinize my coffee habits?"

He couldn't let it go. "That's not coffee. That's a liquid candy bar."

While she tried to pick the best of a dozen different smart-ass replies, his eyes darted down. A pair of officers had just walked in, but she didn't think they'd seen him.

"If I'm seen with you and it gets back to my department, I'm screwed."

His face was taut, the skin barely concealing a square jaw and sharp cheekbones. She wrote for a living, so her mind constantly puzzled over how to describe someone in the fewest possible words. If she'd had only one, it would have been *brawny*. If she'd had three: *brawny, but anxious*. She didn't know what it was, but something simmered beneath his surface. Under that chiseled, carefully cultivated exterior, his anxiety was palpable.

She leaned in. "But you *did* come here, Rob."

Again, she followed his eyes to the counter. The two officers were engrossed in conversation. Hand covering his mouth, he said, "I could be wrong about this, that's the first thing you need to know. If I was sure, I'd…well…I don't know what I'd do. The thing is—"

He paused as a teenage girl walked by on her way toward the bathrooms.

Cole was frustrated. "You said you knew why Ambani was killed."

"I didn't say that. I *don't* know why." He sighed and shook his head in a tight arc. "I really shouldn't be here."

"Look. I don't like being screwed around with. If this has something to do with the story I wrote about you, I—"

"No. That story was BS, but…I just saw you there, and I need to tell someone."

"Tell someone what?"

"War Dog!" The officer's voice came from the direction of the counter.

Warren shot up. "I'm sorry," he whispered. "I shouldn't have come."

Hurrying away, he took the outstretched hand of the officer and shook vigorously. Cole couldn't hear their words from her table, but he seemed to be having a friendly conversation. Apparently he had a switch to flip as well. From anxious cop on leave to back-slapping colleague without a care in the world.

She watched in silence, just long enough to get angry. But she didn't flick the switch to turn on the static. Instead, she bolted for the door, past Warren, and waved down a taxi. She slid in, but a hand grabbed the door as she tried to shut it.

"Wait a second," Warren said.

She looked up from the back seat. "Stop jerking me around, Rob. What the hell is this about?"

He glanced over his shoulder, then squatted behind the door. "I don't want to say too much, but if it comes out that the shooter used a fifty-caliber rifle, that the killing had professional written all over it, and that there's no personal motive, call me. If those three things all come out, I may know something. Something I'm not in a position to tell the department, thanks to you. If not, I'm wrong and this conversation never happened."

The taxi driver looked back. "We going or what, lady?"

Warren slowly closed the door.

By the time the taxi rounded the corner, Cole was dictating her story on the murder of Raj Ambani into her phone.

9

Monday

ROBERT WARREN THREW two quick jabs with his muscular left arm, then a right hook that knocked the heavy bag into his refrigerator. A half-full bottle of Rémy Martin 1738 wobbled on its base, nearly toppling off the top of the rusty fridge.

Warren watched, panting and sweating. Half of him wanted to dive for it, the other half hoped it would shatter on the cracked wooden slats of his kitchen floor. The bottle was a reminder of where he'd been. It represented everything he was now against—his healthy body being the foundation of his increasingly healthy mind—but he left it there to remind him. Of what he'd been and what he'd surely be again if he wasn't careful. The bottle steadied and he went back to the bag as it swung toward him. Another right hook, then a torrent of jabs. Left, right, left, right, left, right. Chest burning, he stopped.

The bolts that held the bag to the ceiling creaked and

the bag rocked back and forth like a pendulum, slowing and finally stopping.

As he cooled down, he stalked from the tiny kitchen through the windowless living room and into the bedroom. From a plastic milk crate—his "bedside table"— he grabbed a tub of grass-fed whey protein and returned to the kitchen. After downing two scoops mixed with organic almond milk for some healthy fat and extra post-workout calories, he stabbed at the screen of his cellphone, which he'd duct-taped to the top of the heavy bag.

Swipe, tap, tap, scroll, tap. It began to ring.

"Hello." The familiar voice. Bright and cheery.

He put the call on speakerphone. "Gabby, this is Rob."

"Rob who? Rob?"

Gabriela Rojas had been his training officer when he joined the NYPD. Coming from the Marines, he'd been embarrassed to take direction from a younger woman. But she'd proven brilliant and tough, more than worthy of the seemingly unending series of promotions she'd received since. From beat cop to sergeant, from sergeant to detective, all in five years.

They hadn't spoken much since he'd left Brooklyn, but Warren trusted her. She was one of the most honest people he'd come across in law enforcement. Had she really forgotten him?

"Robert Warren," he said slowly. "*War Dog*." She'd given him that nickname on day one.

"War Dog? What the hell? It's been like—?"

"Two years."

"Two years. Right. How...how *are* you?"

"You mean the thing?"

"Yeah, the *thing*. We *do* get the paper out here in Brooklyn."

Warren jabbed the bag as hard as he could. "It's crap," he shouted in the direction of the swinging bag. "You know how those people are."

"Dude had it coming, huh?"

Warren walked a square around the bag as it slowed, eyes always on the phone. "In front of an IAB Review Board, I regret my actions. And actually, I *do* regret it. I lost my cool and I'm not proud of it. Off the record? In a city full of scumbags, he may be the worst."

"That bad?"

Warren jabbed the bag again. "Worse."

"Well, it's been great catching up and I—"

"Gabby, what the hell? You, too?"

"You know how it is."

"I'm *that* toxic?"

"War Dog, I'm in the office."

"I get it."

He walked another lap around the bag, the silence thick between them. He imagined Gabby looking over her shoulder in the thinly-carpeted office, his former home in Brooklyn's 72nd Precinct. She was probably afraid someone would hear her say "War Dog" and leak it to one of the cop-haters in the Brooklyn press.

He decided to try small talk. "So how is the 72nd treating you?"

"Huh? Oh, right. I still live in Brooklyn, but I'm JTTF now. You didn't hear?"

It didn't surprise him. New York City's Joint Terrorism Task Force was where Gabby was destined to land. The home of the best of the best. But he'd never expected her to land there so soon. "Whose butt you kiss to get that gig?"

She said nothing, but his off-color joke wouldn't have bothered her. It was something else. One thing about climbers like Gabby was that they knew associating with a toxic cop could land them in a boss's crosshairs and blow torch their careers. He was now one of those cops, and this was one of those times. "Real quick, you got anything on the shooting at the Met? Ambani?"

"Screw off, dude, you know I don't. And even if I did—"

"JTTF not in on the investigation?"

"You didn't even know I was JTTF until thirty seconds ago. Why in the name of Saint Paul would you call me with this shit?"

He went quiet and let out a long sigh. "If *I* knew something, something about Ambani, where would I go right about now?"

Gabby breathed heavily into the phone. "Dude?"

"I'm saying, *if* I knew something, and I am where I am because of the thing, what would you do if you were me?"

"Honestly, I'd either walk to a payphone and call in an anonymous tip, or I'd leak it to a reporter, someone you trust. Let them write it and let us pick it up from there. Either way, I'd make sure my name was nowhere near it. We're gonna catch the bastard who shot Ambani— whether it was a terrorist, a racist, or a jealous ex who hired a pro. When we do, we want your name nowhere near it." She paused. "No offense, of course."

She was right, and it confirmed the instinct he'd had to talk to Cole. The last thing he wanted was to taint the investigation into Ambani's killer by attaching his name to it. And a messy truth about police work was that sometimes it required leaking to the press to get things moving within the bureaucracy. "Thanks, and one more thing."

"War Dog, I—"

"You've seen cases like mine before, so humor me. Please."

She sighed her assent.

"If I don't beat the investigation into my incident, what are my chances at detective?"

"Zero."

"And what are my chances of a lateral move, say back to Brooklyn?"

"Lateral move?" Gabby was whispering now. "Low, but not zero. More likely a demotion. Parking tickets, traffic control. I don't know, stadium work, maybe."

Warren stood in the center of the dark kitchen. The bottle on the fridge called to him, but it had been forty-nine months and fourteen days since his last drink, and he wasn't going to let this break him. He'd changed, and that bottle, still there untouched, was proof.

He ran a finger over the curved lettering on the dusty bottle, tracing the R and the E with his index finger. "Parking tickets? Seriously?"

"Someone's gotta do it, right?"

He walked back to the bag. "Sorry, it's just—"

"I gotta go. Don't worry, War Dog. You'll ride this out."

"Yeah. Catch a couple terrorists for me."

He tapped "End," then laid into the heavy bag so ferociously his knuckles bled. Even if his career wasn't over, it was.

10

Cole squeezed her husband's hand as he pulled her forward, snow crunching under her boots with each step.

"Keep them closed, Monkey Tree. Almost there." His voice brought a smile to her face. It always had.

"Around one more corner," he whispered, his words tickling her ear. "Keep them closed."

Eyes shut tight, she allowed herself to be led forward. "Where are we going?"

"It's a surprise."

She laughed at his childlike excitement. "It's freezing out here, Matty."

"Just a little further."

She knew they were somewhere in Central Park. She'd figured that out from the left turn they'd made out of their building on West 98th Street. But she thought she might be able to figure out where based on sound or smell. Near the carousel she might smell roasted nuts or popcorn from the vendors. Near the reservoir, the sound of ducks.

With her free hand, she pulled her jacket up against the

cold breeze. A whiff of Matt's spicy aftershave hit her. Her absolute favorite smell.

He tugged on her hand to stop. "Open your eyes, Monkey Tree."

She opened them, blinking rapidly as her eyes adjusted to the twinkling lights against the backdrop of darkness. She *was* in Central Park, surrounded by a blanket of fresh snow. In front of her sat a small tree decorated with Christmas lights, ornaments, and old-fashioned silver tinsel. It was a little shorter than her and had been planted in a green plastic tub.

Tears welled in her eyes. "How did you do this?"

He didn't respond. She let go of his hand and walked to the tree, running her hand, still warm from her husband's, across the prickly branches. "It's a monkey puzzle tree?"

"It is."

"And you put it here?"

"I did."

Her first trip with Matt had been to the Pacific Northwest, where Cole had fallen in love with a droopy-branched variety of pine tree that grew in the front yard of their rental. Matt had poked fun at her, calling it "The most ridiculous looking tree on earth," and "God's only mistake." On their last night in Seattle, he'd proposed to her on the Ferris wheel by the waterfront and, after she'd accepted, she'd done a dorky, arm-flailing dance that reminded him of the tree's branches.

Ever since, he'd called her Monkey Tree.

She dove into his arms, then pulled back and kissed him. "Oh. My. God. This is so sweet. But where are we, exactly?"

"North Woods. Somewhere near 108th Street."

"Central Park at night?"

"I figure people can tell I'm a Marine on spec."

It was true. Although forty years old, Matt was built like a tank. Not the kind of guy a Central Park mugger would single out. "How'd you get the lights to light up?"

"Battery buried in the dirt. I petitioned the park for a month, even tried to bribe a guy, but they wouldn't let me actually plant a tree here. Good news is, we can take it home. I thought we'd plan a trip to plant it somewhere upstate, maybe in the spring?"

She kissed him again. "It's perfect."

"Merry Christmas, Jane Cole."

"Jane. Your phone. Wake up!"

Cole shot up in bed, the warmth draining from her all at once. Her phone's triumphant, *Ode to Joy* ringtone filled the room but, as usual, provided none of the advertised joy.

Danny Aravilla sat on the bed next to her, holding her phone in her face. She pushed a tangled swath of hair off her forehead and read the caller ID. "Ugh!"

"Your boss, right? Didn't you say you were on thin ice?"

"Let me *sleep*, Danny." It came out more annoyed than she'd intended, but less annoyed than she felt. They'd been dating for six months and he'd had to wake her up every time she slept over. That was no reason to be pissy with him, though. "Everyone over thirty is on thin ice. If you didn't have a smartphone in your crib, you're always about to get fired."

"C'mon."

"That's how it feels."

He forced the phone into her hand. "Then shouldn't you answer it?"

Silencing the phone, she shoved it under her pillow. "Not taking this call won't make or break me. I'm not supposed to be in for an hour. Max probably wants something new on the Ambani murder. Gave them seven hundred words last night, but since I dared take the evening off from tweeting news McNuggets, I guess he's having a conniption."

"Not that I have much, but I could give you something on Ambani."

"I told you what the rules are. Rules are important to me."

"I know."

Aravilla buttoned the top button of a crisp white shirt, studying himself in the mirror. Cole watched him watching himself. He was handsome, she thought. Square jaw, short brown hair, good skin, lean and toned. His butt looked good in his black slacks. And he treated her well. So why wasn't she into him in any real way?

The answer came as soon as the question entered her mind. *Because he's not Matt.*

Aravilla looped a red tie around his neck. "*Rules* in general are not important to you." He spoke slowly, like he was choosing his words carefully. "You break rules all the time. Jaywalking. Lying to your boss, lying to sources to get them to talk. One outdated journalistic standard is important to you, and that's fine. Just saying, if you *do* get fired, I can help you."

Cole opened her mouth to explode at him, but caught herself in time and took a couple deep breaths. "You're sweet. I appreciate it. There are a few rules that matter, and not sleeping with my sources is one of them."

He swiveled as he pulled on his jacket. "You were sleeping with me before you knew I was a detective. So technically you wouldn't be sleeping with me in exchange for information."

"That's a distinction without a difference."

He shook his head slowly. "Look, stay as long as you want. I know lazy members of the institution formerly known as the Fourth Estate can ignore their bosses and go in late, but central has half the detectives in the city pitching in on this Ambani thing and, if you ask me—"

She put a hand up. "Not another word."

He stopped in the doorway. "You free tonight? I thought maybe we could go on an *actual* date."

Her eyes glazed. Pieces of the dream still echoed like a fading memory. The piney scent of the Monkey Tree, the warmth of Matt's hand. Happiness.

They'd never made the trip upstate to plant the tree. The evening in Central Park had been Christmas Eve, their seventeenth wedding anniversary. Matt left for his third tour in Afghanistan the following week. He died a month later. The tree now sat in the corner of her apartment, dehydrated and clinging to life.

"Jane, what about tonight?"

She didn't reply. Part of her wanted to say, *Go to hell, Danny. Next week would have been my twentieth wedding anniversary and there's no way I'm spending any more time with you between now and then.* She wasn't in love with him, would never be in love with him. But he was a decent guy and didn't deserve her mockery. She grabbed her phone from under the pillow and pretended to be lost in the screen, scrolling.

As he walked out, she looked up.

"See you around, Jane," he called over his shoulder before shaking his head.

She'd known she was bound to disappoint him from the moment they'd met.

11

MAX HERR PICKED up his glasses and pointed them at her. "Try everything. *Everything*."

"I wrote everything I had last night. You think I didn't try every source before I filed? *No one* broke any news yesterday. Not *The Times*, not *The Post*, no one."

"Find better sources."

Her story had been the best she could do, but it wasn't anything special. By the time she'd filed, the police had released a statement indicating that Ambani had been killed by a sniper. Every paper in the city had quoted it. Cole had included Dr. Horowitz's assertion that the fatal shot came from the limestone townhouse, but no one else would confirm it. She'd had very little information about the actual shooting so she'd spent much of the piece on Ambani's background in order to fill column inches.

Cole glared at her boss. Lately, this job had been the one thing she was good at and the lecture left her somewhere between pissed and ashamed. "You and I both know that I have better sources than anyone else here."

"Doesn't mean they're good enough. The best of a bad

lot isn't anything to brag about." Herr stood and walked a lap around the desk, stroking his wizardly beard. "There's gotta be something we can do. Ambani's personal life? His business partners?"

"I'm looking into that, but you think I'm gonna crack this case before the cops? Best chance is we get a leak once they have something."

"Has his wife released a statement or spoken publicly?"

She'd read Mrs. Ambani's statement on Twitter just before coming into Herr's office. "Shocked and devastated. Requested privacy in this time of personal tragedy. Pretty standard, but I have a sense of what she's going through. With a baby coming, I imagine it's...well...as bad as something can be."

Herr ignored her sentiment. "Try. Harder." He flopped into his chair and sighed. "I'm sorry, Jane. I know you're doing your best. We need a win. *I* need a win. I need something no one else has." His face became pinched, as though with pain. "I'm not demanding Pulitzers here, just...a win."

He looked defeated, almost desperate. For the first time in a long time, she felt for him. *The Sun* had lost half their staff over the last ten years. There were rumors of another series of layoffs. Even though Herr did the firing himself, she knew it gave him no pleasure. From the look on his face, it ate him up.

"You're my eyes out there," he said. "You go to Ambani's office?"

"Last night. Total lockdown."

"Okay, what else? Gotta be *something* else."

Cole thought about it again. On the walk to work from Danny's apartment, she'd played her interaction with Warren over in her mind, and one thing stuck out. The story that got him suspended had come out two weeks ago. He'd called *The Sun* dozens of times since trying to refute it, arguing for a retraction. When he'd first approached her, she'd assumed it was about the story.

But he hadn't mentioned it. Not until *she* brought it up, at least. If he'd been obsessed enough about Ambani to approach her, obsessed enough to forget his anger about her story…

It had to mean something. Under normal circumstances, she might have run the interaction by Herr for his opinion. But what if Warren was setting her up?

Herr caught her eye. "I can see the wheels spinning, Cole."

"It's nothing."

"What?"

She nodded at his laptop. "You have Twitter open?"

"Yeah."

"Anything on the gun yet? I checked on my phone before I came in."

He scanned the screen. "Not that I see, but isn't that something you should get from a source *before* it breaks on Twitter?"

"You know how it is on these big murders. NYPD, Feds. Lotta jostling going on behind the scenes. Max, *no one* is talking yet."

Her phone vibrated. She had a notification from Twitter, a direct message from one of her most reliable sources. "Finally!"

Herr walked around to look over her shoulder. "What?"

"Note from a source. Hold on."

@Lebron_GOAT23: *.50-caliber from the rooftop you mentioned. No suspects.*

She couldn't repress the grin that broke out across her face. The anonymous account belonged to Joey Mazzalano, a lieutenant who, despite being a serial sexual harasser and all-around scumbag, had never led her astray. His confirmation that the weapon was a .50-caliber rifle confirmed Warren's suspicion.

"What?" Herr demanded.

"I fed the rooftop thing from Horowitz to my guy and it checked out."

"A rooftop or that *specific* rooftop?"

"Specific. Plus, he confirmed it was a fifty-cal, which I heard from someone else. No suspects."

"Okay, but so what? I mean, go ahead and tweet it, drop an update on the piece from last night, but that's not enough for a full story."

"I might have something else."

"What?"

"Too soon to say, but…" She trailed off. She wasn't yet ready to tell him about Robert Warren.

"Cole, what?"

She hurried from his office, already scanning notes on her phone from her story on Warren. She knew he lived in the Meatpacking District, but couldn't recall the exact address. Minutes later, she was in an Uber headed for his apartment.

12

"WE AREN'T GETTING BACK TOGETHER."

Warren sat at the cracked formica table in his kitchen, but felt like he was floating outside himself, watching his life from above. He called his estranged wife exactly once a month, and for the forty-ninth month in a row, she'd had the same answer.

He put the call on speakerphone, then muted it as she continued. "I just can't trust you, Rob. I don't blame you, but I have to think about Marina."

While she spoke, he pressed his hands to his cheeks and blew out through his mouth violently. He'd read online that breathing this way would calm him down in stressful situations. It wasn't working this time.

"...I can't imagine what you've been through, Rob. And now the story. Marina's not old enough to under-stand it yet, but the Internet is forever. One day she's gonna see it and..."

He unmuted the call. "They're gonna *clear* me, Sarah."

"Even so, you know how papers are. They run the

story on the front page, A1, then they bury the retraction on C29."

"Please, just let me see her. I know I'm not where you need me yet, but I've been sober a long time." He glanced past the heavy bag at the bottle on top of his fridge. "Blood pressure is down to…"

"Down to what?"

He considered lying, but decided against it. "160 over 100."

Sarah sighed. "Are you taking care of yourself? Do you still do that thing where you press your cheeks and blow out air?"

"Sometimes, not usually. I tell ya, I'm mostly better now."

"What did Marina used to call it?"

"When daddy became a tea kettle."

She laughed. "That's right. Look, Rob, I'm proud you're sober. I really am." Her voice was quieter, but also firmer. "And I don't blame you. That stuff with your mom's brother. Your leg. You've got good reasons to be messed up. But that doesn't mean I can let you around Marina. Your apartment is…well…limited, and now you're on leave."

Warren looked beyond his living room through the open door into his bedroom. He could see the corner of the extra-long twin he slept on under a tangle of unmade blankets and sheets. No bed frame, no box spring, just a bare mattress on the floor. Sarah was right. It was no place for his daughter. "*Paid* leave, and I haven't missed a payment. They won't cut my pay unless I'm found guilty, and that's not gonna happen."

"What if it *does*?"

"I could always move back in with you and Marina."

His wife sighed, and he knew he shouldn't have said that. He tapped "mute," sprang from the chair, and threw a series of jabs at the heavy bag.

"Be serious, Rob, and put yourself in my shoes. You could lose your apartment, what little there is of it. If I was with a man like you..."

"Who?" he shouted.

"…You wouldn't want Marina around him."

He breathed a sigh of relief, realizing the phone was still on mute. She hadn't heard.

He unmuted the line. "Are you seeing anyone?" he asked as calmly as possible.

"Not that it's any of your business, but no, nothing serious."

Nothing serious meant she was sleeping with someone. Again, he saw himself from above. This wasn't how his life was supposed to go.

When he'd been honorably discharged from the Marines after losing the lower portion of his right leg, he'd come home a hero. Sarah had gotten pregnant soon after and he'd applied to the NYPD. His life was back on track. The PTSD really got cooking soon after Marina was born. More and more, he'd found himself on edge, though he couldn't have told anyone why. The merest threat provoked a violent overreaction and afterward, shame. Shame that he'd scared his wife, that he'd terrified his daughter. It was like his internal software was corrupted, and he just couldn't march straight, no matter how hard he tried. So he drank, and that mellowed the anxiety, if only temporarily. It blunted his anger, too. But then he needed coke to keep him functioning through the blurry haze of the booze, and that aggravated his temper.

Those days were all in the past—the separation had

woken him up—but the thought of Sarah with another man made the Remy Martin look better than it had in months. He didn't know which he wanted more, to drink it or bash it over the head of Sarah's new lover.

The line did a quick double-beep. Call waiting from a 917 area code—a New York City number that wasn't in his contacts. He was happy to have an excuse to focus on something other than his almost-ex-wife. "I gotta go. Work's calling on the other line."

He accepted the new call without waiting for Sarah's reply. "Hello?"

"Officer Warren, it's Jane Cole. How about we give this another shot?"

"Okay, but I don't see how—"

"Rob, I'm willing to talk about a retraction."

This caught him by surprise, but he didn't buy it. Journalists always had an angle. "Why?"

"I'd really like to talk in person, Rob."

"Why?"

"I'm standing outside your apartment. Buzz me in."

This stopped him. Since the breakup, he'd lived in four different apartments. His new place was a three-hundred square foot sublet, and he was pretty sure there was no official record of his new address anywhere other than with the department. "How do you know where I live?"

"Your wife."

The thought of a journalist talking to his wife made his head feel like it was expanding outward. "You think I'm letting you into my apartment after what you wrote? Please."

"Then come down."

He wanted to say no, but she'd said the magic word.

Retraction. It was the one thing that might give him his life back.

13

"How'd you know about the rifle?" Cole blasted him with the question as soon as Warren walked out of his apartment building.

"Don't you journalists have any shame?" he fired back.

She was used to this. The conflict between police and journalists went back centuries. Maybe it was the timing, maybe it was something else, but this time it felt more personal.

They walked in silence for half a block, Warren shooting angry looks every few steps. Though he limped, his long strides carried him quickly. Cole also walked with purpose, like she was late for something important, so she kept up. They turned west and headed toward the Hudson River, the sun at their backs casting a sharp light on the sidewalk before them.

She was willing to hear him out on the story she'd written, but first she wanted an answer. "Here's the deal—"

"No. Listen. You said you'd talk retraction. I wouldn't

have come down otherwise, and today is really not the day to—"

"*You* approached *me*, Rob. At the Met. You have something you want to say. I was as surprised as anyone that you decided to say it to me, but..." Suddenly, the brick buildings on either side of her seemed to close in. She let out a long sigh. Her mind became a field of gray static. "Oh, what's the damn point?"

Warren stopped a pace ahead, blinking in the harsh winter light.

Without thinking, Cole stopped as well, lost in her internal space. She'd been on this street before. Some club opening, or maybe a friend's birthday party. The details didn't matter. She'd danced with Matt in one of these red brick buildings. The memory had come like a flash, but it was too painful. The static was a reprieve.

Warren eyed her skeptically. "What's wrong with you? Sugar crash? If you avoided empty carbs you'd—"

"It's *not* a sugar crash. Has it ever occurred to you how stupid this little dance is? Cops versus journalists. Journalists versus cops. I mean, we're standing on a vaguely spherical ball of rock, a few dozen elements temporarily pressed into shape, spinning through space around the sun. Two insignificant mumbling sacks of meat, arguing over scraps of information, kept alive temporarily by a literal ball of fire. Makes me not give a shit about you breaking some guy's face, or whoever the hell shot Raj Ambani. And it makes me not give a damn about your paleo-keto-whatever-the-fuck diet that *might* prolong my existence on this shitstrewn rock for a few more years but would *absolutely* deny me the shred of comfort I get from a vanilla latte. Or two."

She thought she saw Warren smile, but he turned quickly and kept walking. She followed.

"'That's BS," he said. "The kind of existentialist crap rich white ladies say when they don't want to be held accountable for their actions."

This jolted her back into the moment. She didn't like the accusation. "You have proof the dust up was anything other than what I wrote?"

"Strictly speaking, no. But I can get proof that will make you understand what happened."

"Did you bash a suspect's face into the grate and break his nose?"

He said nothing.

"Off the record, Rob, just you and me, I swear."

"Yeah, I did, but—"

"Then my story was accurate."

"And circumstances don't matter? Facts out of context are as bad—shit, they're worse than lies. Why don't reporters—"

"I called you for comment on the story. If you wanted to share circumstances or make your case, you had your chance." Jane pushed forward, and the static kept the implications of Warren's argument out of her head. Barely.

He scoffed. "Like you would have listened."

"How about this?" She pointed at him. "You tell me how you knew about the rifle. Tell me what you already know you want to tell me, and"—she pointed back at herself—"I promise I'll look at any proof you have, *and* make my boss look at it. *If* it's real. I'll personally make sure we run a retraction if—but only if—you convince me."

They walked in silence for a minute. Finally, Warren stopped and reached for her hand to shake. "Deal."

"Deal."

His dark eyes met hers as they shook. He looked like he was trying to decide if he could trust her. "I swear, Rob. Convince me, and I'll get the piece retracted." She leaned away and took in his impressive frame. "You're a strong guy, Rob. You hate feeling powerless. It infuriates you that I have this power, but I do." He opened his mouth, but nothing came out. "Now that we have a deal, answer the question. How'd you know about the gun?"

Without hesitation, he said, "I watched the killer buy it."

14

SHE GRABBED HIS ARM. "You what? Start from the beginning."

He tugged his arm free and they continued, turning south on 10th Avenue. "I was on the list for promotion. Detective." He frowned. "I mean, before you took a wrecking ball to my future." His eyes flashed, but he didn't look directly at her. "Because I was on the list, I got invited to a special program where I shadowed teams in each department for a day. Look under the hood, gain perspective. About four months ago I did a day with counter-terrorism. Specifically, JTTF. Even more specifically, a two-man unit focused on narco-terrorism and dark web communications."

Cole knew the dark web was a subset of the Deep Web, essentially a secret internet where people bought and sold drugs, hacking software, counterfeit money, and more. But she had no idea where he was going with this. "Okay."

"This unit was a *Revenge of the Nerds* type thing. I don't know how either of them passed their physicals. The one guy's gut popped out in folds from the bottom of his shirt.

Other dude looked like he weighed a hundred thirty pounds soaking wet. And he was *my* height. But they were smart. Spent their days monitoring postings online. Dark web. Shady stuff."

"What were they looking for?"

"Sales of explosives, passports, safe houses. When they came across kiddie porn or big drug stuff without a terrorism connection, they'd refer it out. One guy monitored public postings. Another did something, I don't know what exactly, but he tried to gain access to TorChats. They weren't supposed to be looking for Arab names, but, c'mon."

"What's TorChat?"

"It's basically a decentralized secure chatroom on the dark web. Good place to monitor the conversations of criminals."

"Okay."

"So they're showing me what they do all day and I get hooked into a thread about guns. Now, I'm a gun guy. Tom Clancy could take notes from *me*, okay? I'm on this thread and a dude is looking for nine fifty-cal rifles, top of the line and customized with a certain type of suppressor. Suppressors are legal, but he wanted something extra. And, of course, he was looking for weapons that were untraceable. The way these things work is you post anonymously, then you can choose to move into a private TorChat with someone to make the deal. Just so happened that I watched this particular deal go down. Nine weapons. Got the sense the buyer was an amateur, at least when it came to his demeanor. He said too much. Didn't say what they were for, but he mentioned NBC's favorite liberal billionaire."

"Ambani?"

"Dude is a regular on their stations. *Was* a regular. Political commentary on MSNBC, hosted Saturday Night Live. Hell, he was a guest judge on The Voice. Being a good-looking celebrity billionaire genius is a pretty good gig if you can get it."

Cole laughed. "What happened with the chat? I mean, what did you do?"

"They couldn't get a trace on the IP address, and it was clear the dude wasn't going to blow up the GW Bridge or anything. They referred it out."

"To who?"

Warren pondered this. "FBI, maybe. Don't know for sure. Wasn't their area, and anyway, a dude trying to buy nine untraceable guns didn't seem to faze them. They saw worse a hundred times a day. I didn't make much of it. The internet is full of political nuts talking about their plots to kill people. And not just the dark web. You can find that stuff on social media or Reddit. Right out in the open. When Ambani went down, though…"

Cole stopped. "Wait. You said he was looking to buy *nine* of the same weapon?"

"I know what you're thinking, and I'm already there."

"If you saw it, surely the *Revenge of the Nerds* JTTF dudes did, too. They'd be following up, right?"

"Like I said, they referred it out. To them, it was one of a dozen deals they saw that day." Warren shook his head. "But damn, I hope someone is looking into it. Thanks to you, I'm not gonna know. I'm radioactive. No one will talk to me."

"So you're talking to me?"

"Right."

"I have an idea, but I'm cold. Can we go to your

place?" He looked at the ground. "Rob, look at me. C'mon. Your apartment's a dump, I get it."

He looked up slowly and she smiled. "I sleep at my sort-of boyfriend's house half the time just so I don't have to clean my apartment. I may not have washed a dish in three years."

He smiled back. "No judgments either way, then. But I should warn you, I don't have any sugar or empty carbs in the place. Lean meats, fresh vegetables, and supplements only. You sure you'll feel safe?"

"Yeah. I think I can fast for a few hours."

15

"JANE COLE." He whispered her name through a mouthful of bologna as he stared at the image on his screen.

Jefferson perked up at the sound of his master's voice.

"Jane Cole."

Jefferson breathed heavily as he walked slowly across the room to stand next to the old man. The old man ignored him.

He'd read every article about the shooting, but the one with the image of a pretty reporter had grabbed his interest. The picture appeared as a thumbnail above the online version of her story, next to her Twitter handle and email address at *The New York Sun*. Shoulder-length black hair, blue eyes, creamy skin.

Like the others, Cole's story had exactly what he expected. He assumed she'd filled it with information about Ambani because the police hadn't leaked anything about suspects. This didn't mean they didn't have anything, but the New York City press was ravenous, and not a single rumor about a suspect had appeared yet.

He reached for his dog's head and pet it softly. "They don't know we did it."

He re-read a paragraph near the bottom.

According to a local resident, who declined to be named, the fatal shot came from the roof of a limestone townhouse across the street from the Met. "Kind of a shallow pop," he said, "not a huge bang." He added, "I was by my window. Heard the shot, looked out, saw a panicked crowd.

The other stories had been more cautious about the exact location of the shot, and no police sources had gone on the record about it. Not that it mattered. He expected they'd figure out the exact location soon enough, and he'd been careful to leave behind no trace evidence. That she'd quoted a neighbor bothered the old man. Had her anonymous source seen more than he'd said in her story? Was he —or she—sharing it with the cops right now? Unlikely, but it was a loose end.

He searched her name, first on the dark web, then on Google. Within minutes he'd pieced together a rough chronology of her life.

Born and raised in New York City, Jane Cole had attended the University of Miami to study journalism. There she'd met Matthew Bright, who at the time served at the Blount Island Command in Jacksonville, Florida. They married soon after she graduated. From there, they'd moved with his transfers: two years at Kāne'ohe Bay in Hawaii and two years in Quantico, Virginia. Finally, he'd been assigned to the 1st Marine Corps District in Garden City, New York. She'd done freelance work as they moved around, and took a job at *The Sun*, where she'd worked ever since.

Matthew Bright had died in Afghanistan three years ago. In the mainstream press, there was a simple death notice and that was all. He opened his encrypted email program.

Dear Mrs. Cole,

I need to know who the source was in your Raj Ambani story. The source who claimed to know where the shot came from. Can you help me?

Anonymous

It was a long shot, of course. Reporters didn't give up sources easily. If she didn't tell him, he would use the death of her husband. But her husband had died in service. He preferred to get what he needed without dishonoring his sacrifice. He'd keep it in his back pocket. He opened the chatroom and typed out a message.

T-Paine: *Brothers, I need information on death of Sgt. Matthew Bright, Andar district, Ghazni province, Afghanistan, February 2, 2016. Details. Personal information. Something I can use to gain leverage.*

He wouldn't have to wait long. If there was anything out there about Cole's husband, his brothers would find it quickly.

16

I NEVER REVEAL MY SOURCES, but thanks for reading The Sun.

Cole pasted the reply from the folder of boilerplate messages she used to combat the never-ending deluge of emails she got from readers.

"What was that?" Warren asked as she pressed *Send*.

"Email. Nutjob wanting to know the name of a source."

They sat at the table in Warren's kitchen, a single light bulb dangling just above their heads.

Cole eyed the dented and duct-taped heavy bag, but didn't mention it. "Rival businessmen, disgruntled employees, personal grudges, extremists. Those are the four categories of possible suspects the TV networks are speculating about. Here." She set her phone on the table. It was open to a clip from CNN titled, *Hunt for Ambani's Killer Begins.*

Warren glanced at the screen, but didn't seem to want to read it. "So what?"

"The clip mentions those four groups, zero specifics, which means CNN is getting generalities from sources. As am I. They're spending more time speculating about racist-extremist groups, even though there's no evidence of that. Hate sells."

"Means nobody knows anything. Nothing worth leaking."

"That means your information about the weapons might be more than anyone else knows. We're both jumping to the same conclusion—nine weapons means this could be just the beginning—but let's look at the other options first. Rival business deals."

Warren asked, "Ambani was in tech, right?"

"He was one of those Mark Cuban kind of guys. I heard about him constantly but didn't know much about his actual businesses. Researched him and found out he pioneered high-frequency stock trading. Became a billionaire early, then started a firm that did all sorts of stuff. Tech, finance, international business."

Warren typed on his phone as she spoke, then held it up. Cole read the headline of an article displayed on his screen. *Critics Say Ambani Deal Would Create Monopoly.*

"I literally just googled Ambani's name with the phrase 'business rivals.' Eight million results, and this was the first one. Something about a deal for X-Rev international." Warren scanned the article. "Hmmm, believe it or not, X-Rev stands for 'Extreme Revenue.' High frequency trading firm working on every major stock exchange. Ambani was trying to buy the company, which pissed off a lot of people. There are quotes from three people arguing that the deal should be stopped. David Swanson from National Investment Strategies, Inc., Ibo Kane from Kane, Inc., Sarah Schwitzer from Gussendorf Analytics. I don't have a damn clue who those people are or what they do, but they sound important, and rich, and they're all quoted in this article saying Ambani shouldn't be allowed to buy X-Rev."

Cole stood and walked a small circle around the table, angling her shoulders to avoid the wall and the heavy bag. "I wonder how a deal like that gets approved."

"I don't know, but you can bet it involves a lot of juice in D.C. An alphabet soup of federal agencies. FTC, DOJ. Those things are all about who you know."

Cole did another lap and let out a long, deep sigh.

Warren said, "No offense, but you look like you need to sleep."

"We said no judgments." Cole stopped at the fridge and pointed at the bottle of Remy Martin. From what she knew, he'd had a bout with alcohol, but was now sober. "Doesn't Cognac count as empty carbs?"

"I keep the half-full bottle there as a reminder of who I used to be. Booze. Other things. Who I'm not going to be again."

By *other things* he meant drugs, but she didn't press him on it. "I'd call that bottle of Cognac 'half-empty.'"

He smiled at the joke. "By the way, what I just said *wasn't* a judgment. Just an observation. You look tired."

"Then your place is a hellhole." She smiled. "Just an observation." She sat. "My boss is in my head, telling me to follow the money, but I don't know any more about those three people than you do. And you said eight million results. My guess is we could find another hundred business rivals. Each one could take a week to look into and I'd be starting behind all the business reporters who know about this stuff. Then there's the weapon angle. Hold on." She grabbed her phone, which was vibrating in her pocket.

The caller ID read, "The Italian Stallion."

She shot a look at Warren. "One of my best sources. Been waiting for this call all day." Before he could respond, she hurried through the living room and shut herself in the bathroom. "What's up?" she whispered.

"You free?" His voice was wet and throaty. It was after five, and this meant he was on the third or fourth pull from the hip flask of Amaretto he carried with him at all times.

"I'm in the Meatpacking District. I'm busy, but if—"

"Got something to show you. You're gonna want to see this."

"Joey, promise me you're not talking about something in your pants."

"You know I only answer to 'Stallion.'"

"Fine, *Stallion*."

"After you see the video I have, you're gonna wanna see what's in my pants."

"Don't screw with me...Stallion."

"I'm on the Lower East Side. Tell me where and I'll be there in ten minutes."

She gave him the address of the bar across the street from Warren's apartment and braced herself internally. Mazzalano was like a drunk, abusive Santa Claus. She loathed every minute with him, but he always came bearing gifts.

17

SHE STEELED herself as he waddled through the door.

In his twenties, NYPD Lieutenant Joey Mazzalano had been a decent boxer, and still clung to his nickname so everyone knew it. After failing at a professional career, he joined the department and rose through the ranks busting low-level mafiosi on the Lower East Side. She'd smelled the corruption on him from the moment they'd met. Now fifty, he was anything but a stallion. Average height, he had a massive square head that was somehow too large for his doughy body. He constantly combed over the few strands of greasy black hair he'd managed to retain, which only brought more attention to it.

He threw his overcoat on a stool and leaned in to hug her. The smell of Amaretto and sweat lingered as he wedged his belly under the bar. "You buying?"

She nodded and he waved down a bartender. "Negroni. And as soon as you see me take my first sip, start making another one."

She leaned away for a breath of fresh air, but smiled politely. "You have something to show me?"

"Always business with you."

"When I'm working it is."

"And when you're playing?"

She grabbed a peanut from the bowl in front of her and shrugged. "I'm *always* working."

The bartender set down his Negroni, a mix of gin, vermouth, and Campari he'd forced her to try the night they'd met downtown at a cop bar. She'd hated it.

Sources like Mazzalano talked to her for one of two reasons. Most wanted something—usually gossip she'd heard on the street, but sometimes information she'd gleaned from within the department. Other sources just liked to talk, to show off how much they knew, or to spread rumors about colleagues. Mazzalano was a combination of the two. Nothing made him happier than knowing something she didn't. He loved to show off what a big shot he was.

But he wanted something from her, too. And it wasn't information.

He'd never let a meeting pass without hitting on her. He was a pig, but that made it easier to work him. Besides that, he was one of her most reliable sources, and Ambani's murder was the biggest story in the country. "You know my policy on sleeping with sources, Joey. I mean *Stallion*. As much as I'd like to, I simply can't." She slid his drink toward him. "Drink up, and show me what you have. On the phone you said it was something big."

Mazzalano let out a hearty laugh. "Something *big*?" He took a long sip of the Negroni, splashing the drink onto the bar as he set it down. "I'm not even going to go there."

He leaned in conspiratorially, sliding his extra-large phone down the bar. He nodded for her to scooch closer. She did, reluctantly.

"This video," he whispered, "has only been seen by a half dozen people. You're the first in the press. And you will *owe* **me**."

"What is it?"

He leaned away and gazed at her with droopy wet eyes. "I said, 'You'll owe me.' Got it, Cole?"

"I always pay my debts."

He pressed play and a video began.

The grainy footage showed ten feet of pavement leading to the side of a building. Attached to the building was a black ladder that stopped about two feet from the ground.

"The alley behind the townhouse," Mazzalano said. "We believe he climbed the ladder to the roof, and that's where he made the shot."

Cole noted that the color of the stone matched the townhouse she'd written about.

After a few seconds without activity, a single dried leaf dropped through the frame, dark brown and twirling slowly until it landed near the ladder. A moment later, a figure appeared from the bottom-left. He walked slowly. Hobbled, actually. And he was bent over at an odd angle, like he favored his low back. He wore a gray hooded sweatshirt and brown pants.

"Moves like an old man," Cole said as he reached the ladder.

"There's not a great facial shot, but there's something coming up."

One hand on the bottom rung of the ladder, the man adjusted something on his back. "Backpack?" Cole asked.

"*Rifle* pack. Ask me, it's the perfect size for a fifty cal."

With great effort, the man swung his left foot up to the

bottom rung, pulled himself up, and climbed. Soon he was gone from the frame.

Mazzalano swigged the rest of his drink and smacked his lips. "Hold on." He scrolled back, pausing the video just as the man pulled himself up with his right hand. "There. It's not much, but it's enough to narrow it down."

Using her thumb and index finger, she zoomed in. The image was blurry, but it clearly showed the side of a wrinkled white face. A thin, wispy beard partially covered a sharp chin.

"Holy shit," she said. "That's the man who shot Raj Ambani. Can I have a copy of the video? I'll tell you where my grandma was born."

Mazzalano's eyes widened and he nodded his assent. For years, he'd noted her black hair and prodded her about whether she had any Italian heritage. He'd do his best Tony Soprano impression, asking "What part of The Boot you from, hon?" A reference to the first episode of the show. Wanting to keep her distance, Cole had always declined to answer.

"My mother's mother came from Sorrento."

"I knew it! But that's not enough. Might give you a copy of the video, but only if..." His meaty hand gripped her knee. Casually, she sipped her wine with her left hand as she tried to brush away his clammy paw with her right.

He held firm and she leveled a glare at Mazzalano. "Stop it."

He closed his eyes and his head rolled back, as if in some kind of reverie. The sweaty warmth of his hand soaked through her pants. His nails dug into her skin through her jeans. "You're hurting me."

Eyes still closed, he croaked, "You owe me. I need this."

She jerked her stool away forcefully, but his grip was so tight it pulled him toward her. He staggered forward, nearly collapsing on her, then fell back into his stool.

"Everything alright?" the bartender asked.

"Fine." Cole straightened her shirt and brushed hair from her eyes.

"Fine," Mazzalano said. "Might'a had one too many." He pulled a black comb from his jacket pocket and made a pathetic attempt to get his greasy hair to cover the expansive bald spot that was the rest of his head. "Sorry. Figured maybe you were just playing hard to get."

Resisting the urge to smash her wine glass over his head, she slid her barstool back another six inches. "Joey, I appreciate the heads up on this. Like I said, I *always* pay my debts. But not in that way. And if you ever touch me again, I'll rip your balls off."

She slapped down a twenty and strolled out as Mazzalano's drunken laughter filled the bar.

18

BACK AT WARREN'S APARTMENT, Cole didn't mention the way her meeting with Mazzalano ended, but she went over every detail of the video.

"I suppose you want to go write about it?" Warren asked when she'd finished.

"Not yet. It's a scoop, but it's not enough." She could win five minutes of fame by sending out a tweet identifying the prime suspect as "older white man," identifying Mazzalano as *a high-ranking member of the NYPD*, as she always did. But she could get a lot more by finding out who the old man was.

"You said sixty-five or seventy? Makes me think..." Warren shook his head. "Nah, never mind."

Cole didn't let it go. "What?"

"We're not supposed to take leaps based on race."

"Cops aren't, but right now you're not a cop."

"Yeah, you think I need to be reminded of that?"

"We're just talking here," Cole said. "Try me."

"When Ambani went down, I thought about that dark web transaction. The nine rifles. The comment from the chatroom: 'NBC's favorite liberal billionaire.' I hadn't given it a ton of thought, but when Ambani went down I realized something. Since that day at JTTF, I'd had a picture in my mind of the kind of guy who'd buy a bunch of specialized fifty-cals."

"And?"

"I pictured a guy like the one you described. Older white guy, probably motivated by extreme political views. The way he decided to do it—sniper-style—it suggests military experience, right?"

"Those are big leaps."

"We're just talking here, right? Plus—"

"Wait." Cole leapt up and pressed her hands into the table. "Going with your theory for a second...the chatroom conversation happened when?"

Warren considered. "Three, four months ago."

"Assuming the guy from the chatroom is the guy from the video, he planned it for months and decided on that particular shot. From a rooftop while Ambani walked into the Met."

Warren looked confused. "And?"

"Maybe the *location* means something. Maybe the... look up how long ago the Met event was announced."

Cole did laps around the heavy bag as Warren went back to his phone.

"Press release from June, so—"

"Six months ago."

"International Wildlife Protection Fund." He scanned the press release. "Huge fund to create international legal standards for wildlife protection." Looking up from his phone, Warren caught her eye. "What are you thinking?"

She leaned on the heavy bag. "If I buy nine weapons from the dark web and plan to take out a famous billionaire with one of them, I do it one of two ways. If I'm a certain kind of terrorist, I strap a bomb to my chest and walk up to his limo as he gets out in front of his house, or his office. If, on the other hand, I want to stay alive, I find a time when he'll be in public and I take him out with a rifle from as far away as possible. I make sure I have a safe place from which to take the shot. My question is this: why is the crummy video I saw the *only* video?"

"You said it was from the alley behind the townhouse?"

"Right, so why isn't there better video from the rooftop?"

"Maybe they didn't have cameras up there."

"Or maybe they were disabled. My point is, if you were planning this killing months in advance, wouldn't you make certain you weren't going to be recorded? Wouldn't you make sure the building was a safe zone?"

Warren stood as Cole sat. He positioned himself in front of the heavy bag and whacked it with a couple quick jabs. "So the question is, who owns the building?"

Under normal circumstances, Cole could get building ownership records in five minutes through a simple web search. The owner of the townhouse, it turned out, was shielded by layer after layer of anonymity.

A public records search told her that the home had been purchased seventeen years earlier by a company called Key One Research. It took her an hour to learn that Key One Research was an LLC formed in Tortola in the British Virgin Islands. As far as she could tell, the company had no American business operations. It's only asset was the townhouse.

It was a shell company, and three years earlier, her search would have ended there.

But in 2016, 11.5 million pages of documents had been leaked from Mossack Fonseca, a law firm based in the British Virgin Islands. The documents, which became known to the public as The Panama Papers, provided the most comprehensive evidence of tax evasion and corruption among the ultra-wealthy that the world had ever seen. The database was online, and there Cole found her answer.

Key One Research had been created by Manhattan billionaire Chandler Price. A call to a colleague at the business section convinced her that Price had purchased the townhouse through the shell company for one of two reasons: to hide wealth from the city and state to avoid taxes, or to separate the asset from his personal wealth, half of which he'd lose in the event of a divorce from his wife, Margaret Price.

From there, the connections had been easy to make. Margaret Price was sixty years old and well known on the Upper East Side for her extravagant parties and her taste for old champagne and young men. She and Mr. Price had been separated for years, but had never formally divorced. For now, she still called the lavish limestone townhouse home. If her Instagram feed was to be believed, she'd been out of town during the shooting. A two-day shopping trip to Paris.

Now all Cole needed was her personal cell phone number. And she knew where she'd get it. "We gotta go to Shooter's."

19

"TELL me again why we're here." Warren unfolded his body to exit the cramped Prius.

The evening was cold and windless, like the air had frozen in place, stinging Cole's cheeks as she followed Warren out of the car. Reaching the sidewalk, they walked toward a windowless storefront. A red awning over a black door read: Shooter's Tavern.

Cole tapped her phone to pay the driver as she spoke. "Because this is where cops hang out."

Warren scoffed. "White cops, maybe."

"You've never been here?"

"When I drank, I didn't drink here. No one I know drinks here."

"Like I said, my cell phone guy is usually here. Dude from the 30th who helps me from time to time."

Cole lead the way in and found them a booth near the front door, the last empty table in the bustling bar filled with cops.

"See him?" he asked.

"Be patient." She scanned the room. "He's not here yet."

"I'm not thrilled about being seen with you."

Cole had noticed Warren tightening up as they entered the bar, and he'd moved to the corner of the booth, where he was least likely to be noticed. "I texted him."

"How long do you want to give him?"

"Until he gets here."

Warren drummed his fingers on the table impatiently. "And if he gives you the number, what, you're just gonna call her?"

"That's my job. You don't get far in this business if you're not comfortable getting hung up on."

Warren chuckled. "I guess cops don't get hung up on as much."

"I guess not. But seriously, the questions are: does she know anyone who fits the description? Was it a coincidence she was out of town that day? Does she have a security system? Does that system include cameras? Does—"

"I get it, you have questions."

"Don't you?"

"Of course, I just don't see why she'd speak with you."

"I have ways of getting people to talk." Cole slid out of the booth. "We might be here a while. I'm gonna get us drinks."

"Mineral water," Warren said.

Cole ambled up to the bar, ordered a double tequila for herself and a mineral water for Warren. Waiting for the drinks, she glanced left down the bar, toward the pool tables in the back. When she saw Danny Aravilla, her heart froze in her chest.

From the booth, Warren followed her gaze. After ordering, Cole had looked left casually, her gaze stopping on a man in the back. He had a pool cue in one hand and his other on the hip of a pretty redhead in tight black jeans.

Warren watched Cole stare at the couple for a full minute. Despite the fact that he was hardwired to dislike her, he had to admit he found her attractive. She had a quick mind and it showed on her face, like a chess player in the middle of a game. Always thinking, always calculating. Despite her sugar intake, she was lean, and her straight black hair and bright blue eyes were a striking, unusual combination.

She dropped a twenty on the counter and, eyes still on the couple, shot her tequila. She returned to the booth without his drink.

"What gives?" Warren asked.

Cole said nothing.

"Is that your cell phone guy, with the redhead?"

"That's my boyfriend." She looked up. "Can we get out of here?"

"What about your cell phone guy?"

Cole sighed. "You know anyone?"

"Possibly."

"Outside you said this was where the white cops hang out. Where do the black cops hang out? Where did *you* hang out before you got sober?"

Warren's shoulders relaxed at the thought of Lady Johnson's. He'd learned in AA that just the thought of alcohol could bring on the physiological state of relaxation associated with drinking. He'd also learned that the best way to stay sober was to eliminate temptation. Don't go to your old haunts, avoid parties with alcohol and, of course, never keep alcohol in the home. He'd done the opposite. If

he could withstand the temptation of a bottle of his
favorite Cognac on the fridge, he could withstand
anything. But he hadn't been to Lady Johnson's in four
years.

"I used to know a guy. Across town. West 30th."

Cole stood. "Then let's go."

The taxi stopped abruptly and Cole slid forward, then
faced him. "That guy in the bar...I'm sorry I got like that.
He and I aren't serious. I just didn't expect to see him there
with another woman."

"Aren't serious, meaning?"

"We haven't put a label on it."

"But you didn't know he was out with a hot redhead?"
As it came out of his mouth, Warren realized that calling
her 'hot' was probably the wrong thing to do. "Sorry."

"Don't mention it. And she *was* hot." Cole sighed. "It's
not his fault. He invited *me* out tonight and I didn't even
respond. I've been terrible to him, stringing him along, not
willing to get serious. He's not a bad guy, but—"

She stopped mid-sentence and looked out the window.
Their taxi had stopped in traffic, the blue and yellow lights
of Time Square flickering off the window.

Warren put a hand on her shoulder. She flinched, and
he pulled away.

"And you're telling yourself you're not jealous," he
said, "but inside you're fit to be tied?" She didn't respond,
and he knew he had it right. "Lemme guess, you've been
single all your life, no kids, career before family, too busy
to fall in love, all that BS women tell themselves?" She
closed her eyes again, and he was sure he had her pegged.

"That's not it," she said softly.

A minute passed in silence. The taxi jerked forward, then turned onto an empty street and cruised.

Cole turned to him. "My husband was killed in Afghanistan."

"*You* were married?"

"Seventeen years."

"Your husband served?"

"Marines."

Warren swallowed hard. "I'm sorry. Really. I lost friends there. I know what it's like."

"Died three years ago." Cole wiped tears on the sleeve of her jacket. "Details were sketchy."

"ISIS?"

"Probably. You were a Marine, too."

"In Afghanistan same time as your husband. Lost my leg below the knee. Honorably discharged."

"I know. That's why you limp."

Warren pulled up a pant leg and flicked the metal prosthetic with his fingernail. "Still scored in the top one percent on the police physical. First amputee accepted for full duty."

"I read about that. Didn't you have to—"

"Raise hell? Sure did. They denied me until I threatened to take them to court." He raised his pant leg more, displaying the spot where his muscular thigh connected to a carbon fibre socket around the knee. "Damn thing gets loose three or four times a day now. Thigh got bigger and the VA won't give me a new one. Got eighty grand I can borrow for a replacement?"

Cole smiled, then sat up straight, as though suddenly realizing something. "Wait, you were in Afghanistan the same time as Matt?"

He'd consoled the widows of friends before, and knew they always wanted more information. "I didn't know him."

The driver leaned on the horn, then swerved around a truck that was blocking traffic.

The flashing lights danced on Cole's pale skin. He'd been wondering about something she'd said earlier. "Your husband dying, that why you seem so, I don't know, depressed?"

"I'm *not* depressed."

"Morbid, then? That stuff you said about sacks of meat and a *literal ball of fire*? Why do you talk like that?"

"That's how things *are*."

"If you ask me, that's pretty damn dark." Warren flexed his biceps inside his shirt, a trick he used to connect with his body, his physicality, before he said something he was afraid to say. "I've been going to church lately, and—I don't know why I'm telling you this—but, well, here we are. Wife tried to make me go every Sunday and I...let's just say if the Raiders happened to be kicking off anytime during the service, I didn't join her."

"That why you two broke up?"

"No. It was because I was a drunk and a coke addict." He'd promised himself to say it out loud whenever possible. Admitting the problem somehow eased the shame. "But what I want to say is, I've been going the last three weekends. Still don't believe anything the preacher says. Still don't know how anyone can take the words in some old book as seriously as they do. I'll tell you this, though: the feeling I get there lifts me when I'm down, calms me when I'm angry. I'm down a lot lately. Angry a lot lately. Community. Emotion. It's like a balm for all the shit in this world, in my life. Ask me, you could use some of that."

The taxi stopped in front of Lady Johnson's, a red brick two-story wedged between much taller buildings. A crowd out front shouted, and a group of smokers blocked the sidewalk. The driver called back to them. "Sixteen-fifty."

"My husband went to church," Cole said. "Lutheran. Loved me even though I never went with him. Somehow he was good enough for both of us."

Cole's hard facade had disappeared, leaving only vulnerability and pain. It was as if it had always been there beneath the cold exterior, but Warren hadn't seen it. He blinked quickly before his own tears could form in response to her pain. He shook his head—like he could shake the feeling out of himself—and reached for his wallet.

Before he could get it, Cole handed the driver a twenty. "My story, I can bill it to the paper."

The professional look returned to Cole's face as she spoke, but now that he'd seen it, Warren could no longer pretend that the pain hadn't always been there.

20

"THERE." Warren pointed to a table at the back of the bar as they entered.

Cole barely heard him over the opening chords of Prince's *Little Red Corvette*, but through an opening in the crowd of mostly black cops, she spotted a man with long dreadlocks sitting alone in the corner. Apparently he'd been drinking a while because three empty shot glasses were strewn carelessly on the wooden table, along with two more full ones and half a pitcher of golden beer.

Warren placed his hand on the small of her back, gently leading her through the bar. "Put your arm around me."

"Why?"

"And don't introduce yourself to anyone."

"What?"

He stopped between two groups of boisterous drinkers, elbows jostling from all sides. "We need to pretend we're a couple. Don't want anyone to know I'm here with a reporter."

Cole slid her arm through the crook in his elbow. "Got it, War Dog."

When they neared the table, Warren glanced down at the man, who sat hunched over a glass of beer. "Davey?"

He said it as though surprised, and Cole went right along with the act. "Who's this, honey?"

The man stood, tossing back his dreadlocks. Short and slight, he looked sickly, with sallow skin and sunken cheeks. Seeing him up close made Cole feel better about her drinking. Though she overdid it on the tequila from time to time, this guy looked downright pickled.

"War Dog?" His slurred words carried a hint of a British accent.

Warren leaned in and one-armed bro-hugged him. The size differential made Cole worry, however irrationally, that Warren might break the drunk man in half. Davey flopped back into his chair. The momentum nearly toppled him over before he righted himself.

They sat across from him, and Warren draped his arm around her. "Brenda, this is my old buddy Davey. Davey, meet Brenda."

Davey reached out to shake her hand, knocking an empty shot glass onto her lap in the process. "Charmed."

"So what's a tiny Brit doing in a cop bar?" Cole asked, setting the glass next to the other empties.

Under the table, Warren flicked her leg, a signal she took to mean, *Knock it off.*

Davey shot one of the glasses of brown liquor. "Drinking, obviously." He turned to Warren. "Thought you'd quit booze and—" he glanced at Cole—"the other stuff."

"I did, but I need something for the lady."

"What's your pleasure, madam?"

Now Cole was confused. "What?"

He patted her hand. "Don't worry, honey." Then, to Davey, "Got any molly?"

"Thought you were a skier."

"Have it or not?"

Davey pulled his dreadlocks into a ponytail and secured them with a rubber band he'd rescued from a small puddle of beer on the table. "You haven't come here in years, you show up with a white chick asking for molly?" He eyed him skeptically. "This have anything to do with your incident?"

Warren said nothing.

"Like maybe you think busting me will get you back in someone's good graces?"

Cole considered chiming in, but this was Warren's turf, Warren's guy.

Warren rested both hands flat on the table. "In thirty minutes, Brenda and me are gonna be back at her place listening to Al Green, if you know what I mean." He shot looks around the bar. "There are at least two other guys in here who can give me what I need. You got molly or not?"

"Sure do, but from what I hear you may not be protecting and serving the good people of New York City much longer, so I gotta charge full price."

Warren's eyes flashed. Cole squeezed his thigh, trying to calm him down.

"Fine," Warren said flatly.

Davey nodded toward an exit door between the restrooms, then slid the beer pitcher toward Cole. "Tell you what, sweetie, you refill my beer. War Dog and I are gonna step out back. Tonight, you'll be rolling all the way to heaven."

He stood and staggered past the bathrooms and through a door marked "Emergency Exit Only." Cole braced for the alarm.

"Disabled," Warren said. "Always has been."

"Should I refill the beer?"

"Nah, just meet me out front in three minutes. And order us an Uber back to my place."

As they left, Cole read the scroll at the bottom of a TV screen over the bar.

NYPD spokesman Todd Framer announced today that there are still no suspects in the Raj Ambani murder.

Leaders from the Indian American Business Association condemned the killing as "possibly racially motivated."

The President called the killing "shocking," "tragic," and "a great loss for American business."

Mazzalano had said that Cole was the first reporter to see the video. The fact that CNN hadn't yet mentioned it confirmed this. If anyone had reported it, images of the old guy would be plastered on every TV screen in the world. For now, it was safe to assume she was the only one with the information. But that couldn't last long.

Behind the bar, Warren found Davey leaning on a dumpster. "Well done, mate. Back home we call it Riding the Train to Cranham—it's the whitest suburb in London. What do you call it here? Jungle Fever? Swap the white powder for a white chick. I guess it's cool, but if you ask me the powder is a more reliable way to feel—"

Warren lunged forward, grabbed him by the shoulders and lifted him a foot off the ground. When their eyes met, he slammed him into the dumpster. A dull, metallic thud filled the alley.

Davey's eyes widened. "I'm sorry...I didn't mean."

Warren let go and Davey collapsed onto the ground by the base of the dumpster.

"Get up."

"You gotta relax, man. You sure going clean was good for you? I was just saying, Brenda's cute. Something different—"

"Get up!"

Davey braced himself on the dumpster, standing slowly. "I'm sorry. I got nothing against…I've got the pills right here, man." He fumbled in his pocket.

"Shut up." Warren leaned in, his face a few inches from Davey's. "Right now, you're going to call whoever you call to get phone numbers. You're going to get me the unlisted cell number for Margaret Price."

"What the—"

"Don't bother objecting. Just do it."

Davey opened his mouth. Warren hardened his gaze, allowed his eyes to fill with rage. "Now." He said it softly but definitively. He didn't want to have to hurt him.

Davey reached into his jacket and pulled out his phone. "No hard feelings. Gimme a minute."

Cole spotted Warren from the back seat as he emerged from an alley.

"Got it," he said.

She smiled. "The drugs or the number?"

Warren flashed his phone at her as he slammed the door and the car took off in the direction of his apartment. It displayed a number with a New York City area code.

"Who was that guy?" Cole asked. "I mean, obviously a dealer, but, why the hell is he getting wasted in a bar filled with cops?"

"Because he's got the best weed in Manhattan and even

cops smoke weed from time to time. He drinks for free, keeps the owner and bartenders supplied, sells to cops. Weed only, unless you're me."

Cole nodded. "He also has phone numbers?"

"He knows a guy who knows a guy."

Cole entered the number in her phone. "How'd you get him to help you?"

"Crooks are always afraid they're gonna get caught. Always. He sold me coke for a few months. He could have gotten me in a lot of trouble, and I could have gotten him in a lot of trouble. He just owed me a favor."

Cole gave him a side-eyed look.

"Slammed him up against a dumpster. Happy?" He pointed at her phone. "Gonna quiz me all night, or call her?"

Cole started the call, but it went straight to voicemail. "Hello, Mrs. Price. This is Jane Cole of *The New York Sun*, please call me back as soon as you can. I know you must be receiving inquiries from every reporter in the city right now, but you'll want to speak with me when you find out what I know, what *The Sun* knows. I won't say too much on voicemail because I respect your privacy. Let's just say it involves a popular television dance competition and an evening you shared with a dance troupe from Japan."

She ended the call.

Warren stared at her, wide-eyed. "What the hell?"

"You don't want to know."

"Oh yes, I do."

The car pulled up in front of Warren's apartment. "You want to come up?" Warren asked as they got out. "I need to hear about the dance troupe."

Cole considered for a moment. "If I come up, I'll probably try to sleep with you. And that's a bad idea for more reasons than I can count. I'm gonna go home."

Warren stepped back. "I'm still married and trying to work it out with my wife."

"I know. That was one of the reasons it would be a bad idea."

"You're damn strange. You know that, right?"

"I used to be less...strange."

"Think Price will call back tonight?"

"I figured she'd be screening her calls, but Margaret Price is a media whore if ever there was one. She'll call."

"You're really not gonna tell me about the dance troupe?"

They moved under the awning of a deli next to Warren's apartment as the rain started. "You've seen her on Page Six, right?"

"I have. She likes younger men."

"And Japanese hip-hop dancers."

"So?"

"Basically she paid for a whole troupe of Japanese dancers to come audition for one of those reality dance shows. Bought their flights, costumes, put them up in her townhouse, the works. Then, well, dot dot dot."

"Dot dot dot? All of them?"

"I wasn't in the room, but one of them gave the story to *The Sun* and, at least *most* of them."

He grimaced. "You'll let me know if you're able to set up a meeting?"

She leaned in and hugged him, her hands tiny against his arms. "I will." She stepped to the curb to look for a taxi, then turned back. "Sorry about what I said. I wouldn't have tried to sleep with you. I don't know why I said that. Next week would have been my twentieth anniversary with Matt. My therapist says I need to move on, but, well, let's just say it's not working. Anyway, I wasn't always this strange."

21

COLE JOGGED ACROSS HER APARTMENT, towel wrapped around her wet hair, looking for her ringing phone. She and Matt had purchased the two-bedroom before his death, anticipating that they'd soon need the extra room for a baby. It felt too large without him.

She found her phone on a table next to the droopy, dehydrated Monkey Puzzle tree. "Mrs. Price, thanks for calling me back."

"With whom did you speak? Shenzo? Damian? Not Uni! I'll murder those little bastards."

"None of them, but I'll be sure to check them out for future interviews."

"Damn you. I thought *The Sun* was a respectable paper." Her tone was haughty, but also loose, like she'd been drinking and was trying to hold it together.

"Look, Mrs. Price, sit with me and my colleague tomorrow morning on the Raj Ambani thing and I'll make sure our gossip guy forgets what he heard about you."

There was a long silence. "You likely already know I was out of town when that monster climbed on my roof and murdered Raj. I supported him, you know. *Knew* him personally. I hosted a fundraiser trying to convince him to run for governor. Gave a million dollars of my husband's money to his little animal project. Anyway, you must know I was out of town." She paused. "You're looking to do a sidebar, right? Beautiful Upper East Side socialite copes with her twenty million dollar townhouse being used to murder a great American? Something like that?"

Cole shoved dirty clothes off the couch and settled into it. "Something like that."

"I could call Max Herr right now." Her tone was harsh again. "There's no way he'd let you run a disgusting rumor about my personal life."

"He already knows, Mrs. Price. And no, he wouldn't run it. He already squashed this one. But our gossip guy could trade it to *The Post* or *The Daily News*. *They* would run it." She paused to let the threat hang in the air. "I can make sure that doesn't happen."

"Fine, fine. I have half a mind to let it run, might be good for my Instagram following. You know, *People* maga-zine says I'm the most-followed woman over sixty. Kids today don't care who you love, but…" she let out a long sigh… "my mother is ninety-one years old and still reads *The Post*. Might stop her heart to learn about Uni or Shenzo. My father fought in the Pacific theater in World War Two, after all. Be here tomorrow at eight."

She agreed, then hung up and texted Warren.

Cole: *Be at the back entrance on the alley side of the town-house at 8:05 tomorrow morning.*

Warren: *Why the back entrance?*

Cole: *I need you there, but there'll be reporters out front. When I break this story, I want you nowhere near it.*

Warren: *Got it.*

She opened her email and read the one from her boss first.

June,

You avoiding my calls? 24 hours without a story, without a call, without a message? What the hell?

Max

She typed a quick reply, assuring him she was close to something big and that she'd be in the office tomorrow. There was no way he'd approve of the tactic she'd used to get Margaret Price to talk. Every paper in New York City traded stories for other stories, traded stories for access. In this case, the gossip reporter had heard about Price's proclivities from a disgruntled lover and never even considered publishing it. But threatening to reveal sensitive personal information when, in truth, she never would have, was a gray area she didn't enjoy spending time in.

She walked to the kitchen and poured herself a full measure of tequila in a Seattle Seahawks coffee mug. Her husband's. Returning to the sofa, she scanned the rest of her emails, stopping on a reply from the anonymous emailer who'd contacted her earlier in the day.

Dear Monkey Tree,

The salutation made her heart skip a beat. No one called her that but Matty. And he never called her that in public. Breath caught in her throat, she read on.

Dear Monkey Tree,

I understand journalists rarely reveal their sources, but allow me to make my case. Your husband, Sergeant. Matthew Bright, died on February 2, 2016 in a firefight in Andar district, Ghazni province, Afghanistan. The details you received were sketchy.

I know something you don't: Matty's body never made it home because it contained evidence of how he was killed. It

*wasn't in a firefight. The men who killed him were never brought
to justice. Deep down you've known this and it's bugged you for
nearly three years. Am I right?*

*I KNOW what happened, and I will tell you. All you need to
do, Monkey Tree, is tell me the name of your source.*

I can meet tonight.

Anonymous

The emailer knew her husband's nickname for her and
he'd referred to her husband as "Matty." Could it be
someone from his unit? Had someone read their emails or
texts? She didn't know, but she couldn't fight the wave of
grief that overcame her.

She shot the tequila, then let the mug and the phone
fall from her hands onto the pile of dirty clothes. Her chest
tightened and she rolled onto the floor, then bashed the
cushions of her sofa as hard as she could. Once, twice, a
third time. Grabbing the cushions, she hurled them across
the room, one into the kitchen, the other two at the door to
the bedroom.

She flopped onto her back in the middle of the living
room, staring at the ceiling, panting. Her eyes went soft, a
blurry field of white that brought the static to her brain.
Outside, the rain pelted the windows. She was empty
except for a single thought: Will this ever end?

The emailer was right. There'd been no body to bury.
Just a sudden break in communication from Matt on a
Monday followed by twenty-four hours of panic and the
arrival of a chaplain and a casualty assistance officer on
Tuesday.

In her grief, she'd read the self-help books and the
blogs. She'd even seen a therapist once a month for the last
three years, as often as she could afford. Following the
therapist's advice, she'd prioritized her physical health. At

forty, she was still in good shape. No one would mistake her for an elite athlete like Warren, but she walked a three-mile loop through Central Park most days and kept the drinking under control. Most of the time. No more than a couple nights a week, and never too much to work the next day.

Her body felt pretty good, but her mind and spirit were a mess. She'd followed the steps prescribed by the therapist. Taken time off, given herself space to grieve, accepted the support of loved ones—mostly through calls with Matt's mother in Seattle. She was the only one of their four parents still living, and the only person who could relate to the pain of losing Matt. The only one who'd loved him as much as she did. The only one who hadn't resorted to clichés—"he's in a better place" or "at least he died serving the country he loved." They'd been angry together, they'd cried together. Through weekly calls, they'd mourned together. But that alone wasn't enough to heal, and the weekly calls had turned to bi-weekly calls, then to monthly calls.

She hadn't spoken with Matt's mother in six months.

She'd read that overwhelming grief can creep up anytime after the loss of a loved one. Purposelessness, emptiness, the feeling that you no longer exist, or wish you didn't. For her, these feelings came with anger. To function, she'd learned to go numb. To embrace the static.

For three years she'd lived between anger and despair. The sudden outbursts of grief were proof that she had no idea what was happening inside her, and never had. Proof that the things she'd known she loved about her husband hadn't even scratched the surface. That an entire hidden relationship had formed between them, a web of intricate ties made of routines and smells and unspoken needs and expectations. A relationship that had lived underneath the everyday.

She only became aware of it by its absence, knowing it was gone forever. What people didn't understand was that, despite being an independent woman, a strong woman, when Matt died, a piece of her stopped existing. A piece she hadn't been aware of. A piece she couldn't replace with positive thinking or a new version of herself.

The death gratuity—the $100,000 the military sent her when Matt died—had helped. She'd spent $80,000 to refinance the two-bedroom apartment his sergeant's salary had helped pay for. It allowed her to stay put on her measly salary, and she'd tucked $20,000 in an emergency fund. She needed the savings in case she got sick, or got fired. She'd told herself it was the prudent, responsible thing to do. But that was bullshit.

For three years, she'd been expecting a calamity, and the money allowed her to drift toward it.

Against her better judgment, she replied to the email.

Convince me you know something I don't, and I'll name the source. Meet me at the Starlight Diner in an hour.

Jane Cole

22

THE RAIN CAME DOWN in sheets, pummeling her wide umbrella as she turned the corner onto Columbus Avenue. Lights from festively-decorated storefront windows illuminated patches of sidewalk, but the streets were empty save for an occasional taxi splashing by.

Meeting random emailers was sometimes part of her job, and she always did so in crowded restaurants and bars, arriving first to control where the conversation took place. Tonight she had fifteen minutes to spare and planned to take a seat at the bar of her favorite diner, where she'd feel safe. Chances were, the emailer was a lonely guy who knew journalists were often the only people who would listen. But somehow he'd learned things about her and her husband. The Marine Corps *had* been tight-lipped about the firefight Matt died in, and part of her believed that finding out the details would put her mind, and her heart, at ease.

Half a block from the diner, a shadow stirred under an awning. She turned toward it just as a hand emerged from the darkness and grabbed her arm. She tried to pull away but was spun around, her wrist twisted painfully behind her back.

"Do not turn around, Mrs. Cole. And do not scream." The man's voice was gravelly and he smelled of wet dog.

Something sharp pierced her shirt and stung the small of her back as she was pushed forward, then into an alley. He pushed her into the wall face-first, her cheek flush against the wet brick.

"Who was the source?"

Before she could think, she heard her voice. "I won't tell you."

"Probably one of those Jew lawyers who own the Upper East Side? Name him."

She said nothing.

"You *will* tell me." He pushed the knife a little deeper. Cole pressed her belly into the cold stone of the building, but there was no further to go. "Who!" he barked, coughing spittle onto her neck.

Revealing her source wasn't an option. "If you knew anything about me, you'd know that I'm half dead inside." Her words surprised her as they came out of her mouth. "To be honest, I don't much care what happens to me. What you do to me. A few things still matter, and not revealing a source is one of them."

The pressure of the knife lessened slightly. There was a long silence.

"Well, I…tell me this then. Did he see anything?"

Cole considered for a moment. He seemed to have moved on from his first demand quickly. In her mind, it clicked. This was the shooter. The man who'd killed Raj Ambani. In the video, he'd appeared to be old, and this man, while strong, had the voice of an old man. He didn't necessarily want to *kill* her source, he only wanted to know if he'd seen anything else, anything she hadn't printed in her story. Anything that could incriminate him.

"You read my story?" she asked, face still flush against the wall.

"I read all the stories."

"And you want to know if he told me any details I didn't print?"

"Yes." He pressed his forearm into the back of her neck, grinding her face against the rough brick. "Now."

"Nothing," she said out of the side of her mouth. "He doesn't know anything other than what I printed."

"How do you know?"

Her instinct to stay alive had kicked in. "It's my job to know. If he heard the gunshot, there's no way he also saw something. I know the window he was standing at and he couldn't have seen anything. Plus, he wanted to please me. That's how I know he told me everything."

The man was quiet for what felt like minutes. Cole stayed still.

"Fine," he growled at last. "In my pocket I have a gun." He tugged her back slightly, fumbled in his pocket, then held a pistol in front of her face. "See! You are going to walk out of this alley without turning around. If you turn around, I'll shoot you. Understand?"

Cole nodded.

He let her go. "Walk!"

She took a slow step, bracing internally. Part of her wanted to turn around, to demand to know how he'd learned about her nickname and what he knew about her husband. But he'd shoot if she turned. Her life would end in the rainy alley.

She took another step, then another, and another,

speeding up as she moved. A dozen paces and she was out of the alley.

She sprinted toward the corner, stopping outside under the bright light of the Starlight Diner sign. She pulled off her jacket, then slowly rotated it, studying each sleeve, then the front, and finally the back. The silver light flickered off the shiny blue fabric. On the bottom hem, below the small hole left by the knife, she saw it. A single hair, stuck to the slippery fabric. She pulled it off, then stuck it to a business card from her wallet.

Next, she called Joey Mazzalano.

23

Tuesday

COLE RAN a finger over the patch of rough skin on her cheek, re-living the sensation of being pressed into the wet brick wall. Baggy-eyed and still shaken, she swung her feet onto the seat of the taxi and opened YouTube. She had fifteen minutes to cram for her interview with Margaret Price.

She'd met with Mazzalano for twenty minutes the previous night and, for the first time ever, he hadn't hit on her. Mentioning that she had DNA evidence from Ambani's killer was enough to make him focus his energy above the waist. She'd considered calling 911, but going straight to The Italian Stallion was a sure way to avoid hours of repetitive interviews that lead to nothing. Plus, she'd promised to pay her debt, and now she had. Mazzalano had promised to lean on everyone he knew to get the DNA lab to run the sample quickly, but it would still take a couple weeks. They made a deal: he could use the information however he wanted, as long as he gave her the scoop.

She'd been home by 3 a.m., staring at the ceiling from the bed that filled most of her small bedroom. She'd considered writing a story on her encounter, but without a description of the man or any update from the police, she had nothing worth writing.

As the taxi crossed the park, she clicked on an interview with Margaret Price, a stand-up on the red carpet of a charity event hosted by Troy Murphy, an actor Cole had never heard of.

A young interviewer shoved a microphone in Price's face. "What inspired you to come out in support of this cause tonight, Mrs. Price?"

"Giving back is very important to me, always has been. And the people at Refugee International are doing important work." Her voice oozed self-importance, as though the listener should be paying by the minute for the privilege of hearing her words.

"I have to ask," the interviewer said with a sly grin, "is it true that you and Troy Murphy are dating?"

Price's head tilted to the side and she touched the lower half of her throat. "Not at all," she said. "Troy is a good friend and I respect the work he's doing with Refugee International. That's all. Find someone else to gossip about."

Cole closed the video and opened another, a sit-down promoting a cosmetics line she had endorsed in the early 2000s, when she was still living with her husband. Nearly twenty years ago, Cole thought, and her face looked exactly the same. This time, she watched the video on mute, focusing on Price's hands and face. Three minutes in, she saw what she was looking for. A hand to the neck.

She rewound the video fifteen seconds and listened to the question.

"Mrs. Price, you've never endorsed a line of cosmetics, you've never endorsed any product at all. Why now? Why Allure Natural Cosmetics?"

"Thanks for asking, Tiffany. I endorsed Allure because I believe in the products. I use them myself every morning and evening…" her hand moved to her throat… "and they've simply revolutionized my daily beauty routine."

Cole shoved her phone into the back pocket of her jeans as the taxi stopped in front of the townhouse. She didn't know whether Margaret Price knew anything about Ambani's murder, but she now knew how to tell when she was lying.

Cole rushed past a small group of reporters lingering in front of the townhouse, then rang the doorbell. A moment later, a young Asian man in a crisp black suit answered. "My name is Uni. I am Mrs. Price's assistant. I presume you are Jane Cole?"

She considered a dance-troupe joke, but thought better of it. "That's me."

She shot a look at the jealous reporters over her shoulder as she followed Uni into the two-story entry hall. Uni closed the door behind them, then led her into a large living room, nicely appointed with modern blue and white furniture, but not lavish in the way Cole had anticipated. She'd expected an old-fashioned elegance, but the house looked like it had been furnished by an upscale Ikea for rich people.

Margaret Price sat on a chaise lounge in the corner.

"Jane, welcome. Would you like something to drink? I'm having tea, but Uni can make anything you like."

Uni looked at her, one eyebrow raised.

Cole waved him off. "I'm fine, but I have a favor to ask. In a few minutes, my associate will appear at your back door. Please let him in."

"Why didn't he come in the front with you?"

"Reporters."

"If he's your associate, isn't *he* a reporter?"

"Not exactly. He's a cop."

Price sat up a little straighter. "But why? Surely the—"

"Don't worry, it's not that. No one suspects you of anything. It's for my story. He was nearby on the day of the shooting."

The argument didn't make much sense, but Price didn't question it. "Fine, fine then. Uni, let him through the kitchen door."

Cole sat in a chair across from the chaise lounge and cleared her throat awkwardly as she contemplated the best way to approach Price. "First of all, thank you for seeing me, Mrs. Price."

"Call me Maggie."

"Thank you, Maggie. And I'm sorry for the unusual entry of my friend…oh here he is."

Warren entered, trailed by Uni.

Price studied Warren. "Oh, yes indeed. Men like you inspire me to give money to the New York City Police Foundation every year. If only they'd let me stuff my checks into the back of his trousers. Turn around honey."

Cole stifled a laugh. "Please, Maggie. He's a former Marine. Have some respect."

Price growled seductively. "The few, the proud." After an awkward silence, during which her eyes never left

Warren as he took a seat next to Cole, she said, "Right then, ask your first question, Mrs. Cole."

Cole launched a pre-planned series of questions about the building. How long had Price lived there? How did she like the neighborhood? Small talk. Questions to which Cole already knew the answers. This was a tactic she used often with tough interviews. Get them talking about easy stuff to lay the groundwork and get a read on them. If she was lucky, Price would lie about something Cole knew the truth about, allowing her to test her tell.

But she didn't lie, so once they established a rapport, Cole shifted gears. "What were you doing on your trip at the time of the shooting?"

"Shopping. Nothing like Christmas shopping in Paris."

Had she tilted her head slightly as she answered? Cole wasn't certain. "Find anything nice?"

Price frowned. "How can this possibly be relevant to your story?"

Cole flicked the internal switch, turning off every part of herself except the amorphous static interior. Her eyes focused on Price like a laser. "Did you leave town because you knew Raj Ambani would be murdered from your rooftop?"

Price gasped. "Good Lord, no!"

She spoke the truth. Cole was sure of it. It would have taken a better liar to respond so immediately and authentically. "Did someone suggest that you leave town at that time?"

She hesitated half a second and steadied her eyes on Cole. "No!"

There it was! Just as she spoke, Price brushed her neck softly with the back of her fingertips. "I go to Paris in the winter. Every year. The new styles come out there months before they hit New York and—"

"Who suggested those *exact* days?"

"I just told you." Price's hurt look was quickly replaced by an imperious glare. "No one suggested anything. Uni, please see Mrs. Cole out."

Warren wordlessly placed his body between Uni and Cole.

Cole stood and leaned into Price's face. The socialite's skin betrayed the tightness of a recent botox treatment. Her makeup was a thick shade of tan that looked unnatural close up. The room faded away and Cole's awareness shrank until it contained only Price's well-preserved face, awash in a sea of gray. "Mrs. Price—Maggie—just one more question. Did your husband tell you to leave town on those particular days?"

"Uni, please make them leave."

"Did he?"

Price's neck flushed crimson and she fanned it with both hands. "Please leave."

Uni maneuvered around Warren and grasped Cole's forearm. She immediately shook herself free. "It's okay. You answered every question I had." She faced Uni. "We'll see ourselves out."

24

Outside, Cole slipped on a pair of sunglasses as they walked through puddles that steamed and sparkled in the bright morning sun. They passed the Met, open again as though nothing had happened, and entered Central Park at 84th Street.

"How'd you know she was lying?" Warren asked.

Cole didn't respond. She was coming down from the intensity of the confrontation with Price. Her nerves were fried.

"You look...shook. Tired. Surely Maggie Price didn't rattle the great Jane Cole. What's going on? And what's that mark on your face?"

"You should see the one on my back."

"What?"

She let out a long sigh. "Last night I met the man who killed Ambani. The man from the video."

"What?" Warren grabbed her by the shoulder to force her to stop walking.

Her hands quivered. "He sent an anonymous email. He

knew stuff about me—about Matt. His death." She hadn't told Mazzalano these details and they sounded unreal as she said them out loud. She sniffled. "He knew details and I—"

Warren's eyes widened. "Holy shit. You're serious? Did you talk to the police? Jane, tell me what happened."

She began walking again and, for the next ten minutes, she talked through the events of the previous night. "They're not gonna be able to find him from the email," she concluded. "Any guy with a decent laptop can run anonymization the NYPD can't track. And I didn't look back. Lieutenant I know is gonna rush the DNA sample, but..."

"Yeah, that could take weeks."

She shook her head, frustrated. "Damnit, I *should* have looked back."

"No, you *shouldn't* have. Remember what I said. This thing had 'professional' written all over it. If that's what he is, guys like him genuinely don't want to kill innocent people. But he would have. You did the right thing."

"I can beat myself up about that later. Can we talk about Chandler Price? I had a hunch, and Maggie confirmed it."

"Tell me how you knew she was lying?"

"Most people have a tell when they lie. Looking at the ground, over-explaining, offering too many details, shifting their eyes. You can learn all that with a Google search. Takes a while to get good at it, though. Takes a lot of self-control to really be *with* the person, rather than in your own head. I'm a reporter. People lie to me all day, every day. Helps to be able to know when. Maggie's tell was easy. She brushed her neck. People feel vulnerable when they lie. Some protect vulnerable body parts unconsciously."

"But how'd you know about her husband?"

"She was telling the truth about not knowing Ambani would be shot. But *someone* did. My guess was that whoever that was, they got her to leave town those days." She shrugged. "Chandler Price still owns the building, still pays the bills. My hunch was that he was the only person who could get her to leave the house on those specific days. "

"Pretty sure she wasn't in on it?"

Cole nodded slowly. "I wondered whether her husband had a business deal with Ambani that went bad, or maybe they had a mistress in common."

"Ambani was happily married, from what I've read. Plus, why nine rifles then?"

"Don't know, but let's look into the business angles first. Low-hanging fruit."

They stopped at a bench beside a large muddy field. Cole crossed her legs and folded her heels under her hamstrings. Warren began a series of searches on his phone, combining the names Raj Ambani and Chandler Price. Together they read a few of the links, but the quick search didn't bring up any obvious connections. Warren kept searching while Cole called Chandler Price's office number. The man who picked up told her in no uncertain terms that he hadn't given an interview in three years, and there was no chance he was going to change that policy today.

"Should we try for his cell number?" Warren asked.

"Maybe, but my hunch is that he's a lot smarter than his wife, less likely to answer his own phone. And what his secretary said is true. He doesn't give interviews. Even if we get him on the phone, he'll just hang up on us. Maggie craves the limelight. He avoids it."

Warren nodded down the path. "Let's walk."

"We don't have much," Cole said. "So let's do an experiment." As they walked, she did an image search for Chandler Price and held up the first picture to Warren. "Would you say he looks more like an Oompa Loompa or an over-steamed dumpling?"

"You must be a writer. I was just gonna say he looks short, pink, and sweaty. What else do you know about him?"

"His *darling* wife was involved in all sorts of charities, mostly liberal stuff, Hollywood stuff. She liked hanging with A-listers."

"If I had my cop hat right now, I wouldn't want to speculate. But I don't, so I'll just say it. From the moment I saw the post about the weapons, I thought it was some ultra-nationalist thing, maybe even a white supremacist thing."

"Last night in the alley, the shooter asked me whether my source was a Jew. Said it with loathing."

"So let's run with that," Warren said. "Let's say it's *not* a business thing, but a political or racial thing. Chandler Price wants Raj Ambani dead, he gets this old dude to buy the weapons, then makes sure his wife will be out of town."

"Then he disables the video security on the townhouse, giving the guy the cover he needs to get up to the roof from the fire escape, take the shot, and escape clean." Cole swerved to avoid a rollerblader. "That's it."

"What?"

"You just said it. 'He gets this old dude to buy the

weapons.' If that's true, there's a paper trail. A *money* trail. It's the oldest cliché in journalism. Follow. The. Money."

"It's a cliché in police work, too, but it's a cliché for a reason. It works." They turned back in the direction of the Met. "But even if there's a paper trail showing the transaction, I couldn't get those even if I was still a cop." He stopped short and faced Cole. "But I know who can."

25

AN HOUR LATER, Cole and Warren exited the elevator at the 23rd Street entrance of The High Line, a public park built on a one-and-a-half mile elevated rail structure running along Manhattan's West Side. The trees and bushes sparkled with Christmas lights. Red bows were tied around the garbage cans that dotted the pathway every few hundred yards.

"Who are we meeting?" Cole asked.

"Better if I don't say too much."

"Why are we meeting *here*, though?"

"'Cause this is the last place I'll run into someone I know on a cold December afternoon."

They crossed a frozen lawn and sat on wooden steps that dead-ended at a stone wall. The park was deserted.

"In the summer," Warren said, "this is a great spot for picnics. It's packed. Today it's a good place to get a cold ass."

Cole scooched out of the puddle she'd sat in. "Cold and wet."

"There." Warren pointed at two men approaching from the south.

They were young, late twenties or early thirties, and not in uniform. One was tall and rail thin, the other short and dumpy. Why did she think she recognized them?

"Digital JTTF unit," Warren said before she could ask who they were. "Guys I told you about. Fat pasty dude is Samuel Bacon. Tall black dude is Norris Ubwe."

Ubwe approached Warren, ignoring Cole. Bacon stood behind him, looking around nervously. "What is this about?" Ubwe asked. He appeared to be the leader.

"You remember me?" Warren asked.

"Yes, I do, as I said on the phone. Who is she?" He spoke by-the-book English with a slight Nigerian accent.

Cole extended a hand. "Jane Cole, *New York Sun*."

Ubwe took a half-step back. "You brought a reporter?"

Warren smiled. "She's an expert in breaking stories about critical failings within the NYPD. *And* the JTTF."

Bacon stepped toward them, a look of recognition passing over his face. "Wait, isn't she the one who wrote about *you*?"

Warren grinned. "Ruined my career. So you gotta be wondering why I brought her here."

They nodded in unison. "When I worked with you two that day in JTTF, we saw a post about a man seeking nine weapons. Do you remember?" They nodded again. "You refer that one out?"

"Probably," Ubwe said. "FBI, most likely. I don't remember for certain, but that is protocol. I can check."

A cloud passed in front of the sun and a light drizzle started to fall. "I don't like being cold," Warren said. "So I'll make this short. We believe the man who sought those weapons used one of them to kill Raj Ambani. And unless you want *The New York Sun* to print a story about how you guys blew that one, you're going to help me. Deal?"

The two men exchanged a look, then Ubwe nodded.

"I'm glad." Warren reached in his pocket. "There's a name on this piece of paper, with a couple known addresses. I need his bank records for the last year. All of them. I need them emailed to the address that's also on that piece of paper. Within an hour."

"But that's illegal," Bacon said.

Warren ignored him. "You can get them off the dark web, I assume."

"Maybe, but we might have to hack into—"

"I don't care how you do it, but do it from a home computer. I don't want you getting the department mixed up in this." He looked from one to the other, his gaze cold as ice, then took Cole by the hand and led her back to the elevator.

When the email arrived, Cole and Warren were finishing lunch at a diner in the West Village. It came in the form of four PDFs, one for each of Chandler Price's bank accounts, ranging from thirty to over three hundred pages.

Warren forwarded the first two to Cole, who opened them on her phone. "When you have as much money as Price, there are going to be a lot of transactions. Start with today and work backwards. Look for anything unusual. Large cash withdrawals or transfers. If we're lucky, personal checks."

They worked in silence, Cole scanning two of the bank accounts, Warren scanning the other two. After a few minutes, Cole said, "Here's something. A regular payment of $4,000 to Maria Flores."

"Address?"

"No, and there are probably a hundred Maria Flores' in New York City. We could spend a week looking for her."

Warren looked up. "And it's probably a mistress he's paying off, anyway."

"Could be the wife or partner of the killer. Maybe they sent the money through her to hide it?"

"Possibly, but if I'm right, this guy doesn't have a wife, doesn't live with a woman. We're looking for a sad old white man in his seventies. Probably ex-military."

"What about this?" Cole said. "Transfer to a guy named Michael Wragg for $25,000 three days ago. This was from Price's Delaware Trust account."

"That name...I saw that name."

Warren scrolled furiously through a PDF. "Here. Michael Wragg. A payment for $99,000 on September first. That's right around when I saw the weapons post."

"That sound like the price of nine custom, untraceable rifles?"

"Sounds about right."

Cole tapped her phone. "Already searching for his address. Two Michael Wraggs in New York City. One in the Bronx. One on the Lower East Side."

Warren jumped out of the booth and threw on his jacket. "Then what the hell are we waiting for?"

26

MICHAEL WRAGG LOGGED onto TorChat as Jefferson whined in the corner.

Since his visit with Jane Cole, he hadn't left the house. She'd convinced him that her source hadn't seen him, but someone else might have. He was willing to go to prison for what he'd done, but there'd been a delay in the mission. Now he feared that if he was arrested before it was complete, he'd be tortured until he gave up his brothers.

He scanned the latest comments in the chat window. Two of his brothers were in the middle of a debate.

Kokutai-Goji: *The shot wasn't possible. We didn't anticipate the last minute protocol change. The Silver Squirrel will die tonight.*

Tread_on_This!: *I could have made that shot!*

Kokutai-Goji: *No one could have made the shot. We decided to hire the best, and I did.*

Tread_on_This!: *You screwed this up Kokutai-Goji. Now we're off schedule.*

Kokutai-Goji: *It couldn't be helped.*

Tread_on_This!: *You sure tonight will happen?*
Kokutai-Goji: *The Truffle Pig assured me.*

He wasn't their leader, but he thought of himself as the elder of the group even though he'd never be certain about who was on the other end of the chat. He didn't know the ages or real identities of his brothers. But they seemed young, impatient. Probably millennials. As usual, he'd need to be the voice of reason.

T-Paine: *Brothers, let me explain something to you.*

Jefferson yelped at the window. He jammed his nose into the small crack, as he often did when Duc was emptying fish bones into the dumpster below. The smell was stronger than usual today.

"Shut up! You're not getting any damn fish."

Jefferson clawed weakly at the window and yelped again.

The old man limped across the room, took a slice of bologna from the fridge and threw it toward the dog. It stuck to the window and slid slowly to the floor. "There!"

Jefferson pawed the meat, sniffed it, and again stuck his nose under the window, whining for the succulent bones below.

"Shut up!"

The dog stared at him with tired eyes, then pawed at the window, scratching it with his nails. Wragg grabbed the baseball bat from the glass case and lunged toward Jefferson, swinging the weapon a couple feet above the head of the cowering dog. Breathing heavily, the old man stared at Jefferson until he was sure he'd shut him up. He returned to his laptop and placed the bat back on the desk. He needed to get his brothers back in line.

T-Paine: *We can't allow infighting to derail us. We are very different men, so we are bound to disagree from time to time.*

Our brother Kokutai-Goji tells us The Truffle Pig was not able to take the shot at the appointed time, and even the lying media reported a change to The Silver Squirrel's schedule. Remember, we hired The Truffle Pig because he's a better marksman than any of us. If he says the shot wasn't possible, it wasn't. Everyone else, adjust your plans by one day. Make it work. Remember why we're doing this.

He stared at the chat box, waiting for replies.

Gunner_Vision: *T-Paine is right. Stay focused on the mission, adjust plans as needed. This is only beginning.*

It's_Our_Country: *Only beginning. The world doesn't know yet what we have in store.*

8/15/47: *They will soon.*

Gunner_Vision: *T-Paine, we've all been following news reports, for what they're worth. It seems like you're safe. How does it look from your end?*

T-Paine: *Had a slight hiccup with a potential witness, but it turned out to be nothing. FBI or CIA or NYPD could break my door down any minute, of course, but I believe I'm clear. And even if they do, it won't matter. You all know what to do.*

In the corner, Jefferson whined. The old man shot him a contemptuous look. "You're a weak old mutt. I really should have named you *Hamilton*."

Jefferson barked at the window and the old man grabbed the baseball bat from the desk. Stalking across the room, he cocked the bat over his head.

He stopped when he heard the scratchy *bzzzzzzzzzzz* of his door buzzer.

27

COLE AND WARREN waited in front of the faded red door. Warren pressed the buzzer again. A minute passed, then two.

On the ride over they'd done a series of searches for Michael Wragg and found nothing online or in any of the databases Cole could access from her phone. No arrest record, no mentions in the press, and no record of property ownership. Cole always started her research with an internet search and she'd learned that there were a few sharp dividing lines based on age. Young people were all over the internet, mostly social media platforms like Snapchat, Instagram, and Twitter. People in their forties and fifties usually had Facebook and LinkedIn profiles, while people in their fifties, sixties, and seventies were more of a crapshoot. Some had online profiles. Others had no internet presence whatsoever.

That didn't mean Wragg wasn't their guy, of course. If their guess was right—that Michael Wragg was the man who'd purchased the guns on the dark web—he was likely smart enough not to leave any trace of himself online under his real name.

"What the hell were we thinking?" Warren asked.

Cole mashed the buzzer again. "There was a chance he'd be home. If he had the guts to meet me last night..." She trailed off, studying the buzzers of the other apartments.

Warren followed her eyes. "What?"

"There are three floors, two apartments per floor. As a journalist, there's nothing wrong with me buzzing the other apartments and asking the residents a few honest questions about their neighbor. He's not online, at least not under the name Michael Wragg, but if he lives here—"

"Oh, hell no."

"Why not?"

"Uhh, like ten reasons. You might run into him in the hall. You might tip him off that we're here. Speaking of that, why *are* we here? What the *hell* was I thinking?"

Cole frowned. "You're right. *I* should be here. You shouldn't."

"You think I'm gonna leave you here alone?"

Cole stepped back from the door. Across the street, there was a bar with a table in the window. She nodded at it. "Buy you a shot while we talk this through?"

He gave her a sideways look.

She raised her hands in acquiescence. "Sorry. A shot for me, coffee for you."

Wragg caressed the baseball bat and stood by the door as the echo of the buzzer faded. "They're gone." He cursed himself for not installing a video doorbell. He'd tried to convince the landlord to do it, but he'd been too cheap to pay for it.

He paced to the window and looked out. The fire escape was empty. The alley was empty. He hadn't eaten in a day, and the scent of fish bones that wafted up—carried by steam from a vent—made him salivate.

Jefferson lay silently on the floor by the window.

"It wasn't the police," Wragg said to the half-dead dog. "They wouldn't have used the buzzer. Probably a salesman or a wrong address. A teenager pressing all the buzzers."

Back at his desk, he used his cellphone to dial Trần's. "Duc, it's Michael from upstairs…I'll have the usual… Fifteen minutes, yeah…What?…No, I don't need any bones for Jefferson." Wragg glared at the dog. "He's been bad."

Cole sipped tequila while Warren warmed his hands around a coffee mug. They sat on the same side of the table in the window, watching the red door across the street through sheets of icy rain.

"I should call this in," Warren said.

"You mean Wragg, the financial transactions?"

"Not that. Can't tell anyone how we got that information. I threatened those guys but there's no way I'd ever out them on this. We have no good reason to be here."

Cole slid her shot glass back and forth on the table. "That's where cops and journalists are different. I didn't break any laws to get that information. Maybe you did, but I didn't. And the First Amendment protects me. Once the information is stolen, I can legally publish it."

"That's pretty messed up."

Cole shrugged. "Be that as it may, it's the law, at least according to the Supreme Court."

"What about an anonymous tip? We call in with the name Michael Wragg and the address, say he's connected to the Raj Ambani murder?"

Cole shook her head. "Fine, but your buddies are getting a thousand tips a day. Maybe they get around to checking him out. Maybe they don't."

"That's not how it works. They might already be on to him."

Warren swigged his coffee.

Cole shot the rest of her tequila, eyes glued to the red door. "How's the coffee in this joint?" she asked.

"Burnt, which is how I like it." He waved at the bartender, who brought over the pot and refilled his cup.

"You like burnt coffee?"

"Same with my burgers. Burnt like a hockey puck."

She smiled, her eyes on the red door. "That's sacrilege. Matt would have booted you out of our kitchen if you asked for meat any way other than medium rare."

"I like my meat like I like my enemies. All the way dead."

She chuckled, then turned to him, watching as the steam from his coffee clouded his face. The Warren she was coming to know was definitely angry, but he was a serious cop, as interested in getting at the truth as she was. "Convince me. About the suspect."

Warren waved her off. "Doesn't matter anymore."

"It does. If I got it wrong, I want to know. *Need* to know." She stretched her arms over her head. The tequila made her feel loose. "But I don't think I did. You already admitted it."

"Context."

"Give me a context that justifies what you did."

He sipped his coffee, considering this, then shook his head sadly. "There isn't one. I was in the wrong."

Cole opened her mouth, ready to argue, but nothing came out. His face seemed to have softened, like all the tension had dropped from it in an instant.

Warren slid his chair closer to hers. "I was wrong. I mean it. But if you want, I'll show you the context."

"Show me?"

"I have video."

"Why didn't you…what?"

He put his hand on hers. "I'll show you, but Jane, this is serious. This has to be one hundred percent off the record, okay? I'm not supposed to have this. The person who sent this wasn't supposed to send it. She could go to jail for sending it."

"Off the record, sure."

He lifted her chin and looked right into her eyes. "Jane, do you swear? I want you to see this. To understand. Maybe it will come out one day, maybe not. For now, no one else can know. "

She swallowed hard. "I swear."

Warren opened his text app and scrolled for a moment, then tapped on a video clip. It was dash cam footage, a wide angle looking into an empty police car at night. Blue and red lights flashed from a police car out of frame, giving the video an eerie feel as the interior of the car brightened and darkened with the swirling lights.

A man appeared on the bottom right of the video. Cole recognized Warren's muscular torso but his head wasn't in the shot. Another head was. A rear door opened and Warren pushed a man into the back seat. He was around thirty, with greasy blond hair, a pockmarked face and a crooked nose that looked as though it had been broken several times.

Once the man was in the seat, Warren closed the door, walked around to the driver's side, and got in. In the back, the man wore an odd, serene smile.

Cole paused the video. "What was he arrested for?"

"We had him on child porn charges. When we got to his apartment, we found…"

"What?"

"You don't want to know."

"Context, right? Don't I *have* to know?"

Warren's lips quivered and his eyes got hard. "Found a nine-year-old girl"—Warren sniffed—"chained to a bed. She turned out to be Vietnamese, sold to a trader by her father when she was seven. Took her a week to say anything, and the only English phrase she knew was, 'Yes, sir.'" Warren looked down at the table, as though he was trying to hold it together. "He'd *trained* her. This wasn't in Iraq or some brothel in Thailand. This was in Queens. In 2018. In our city this is happening right now."

Cole felt sick.

Warren pointed at the top of the screen. "Even cops have to pay tolls. I had my wallet out and left it open on the dash. That picture is Marina, my little girl. Five years old."

Warren started the video, which showed him starting the car and turning to look for traffic. He pulled out, but as he sped up his wallet flew off the dash and appeared to fall between the seats.

"My wallet fell open," Warren said. "He could see the picture."

The man in the backseat called out, "Hold up."

"What?" Warren asked, turning.

He nodded at the wallet. "That your baby girl?"

Warren ignored the question.

"She's cute. What is she four or—"

"Shut up." Warren's voice was low and slow.

The man licked his lips. "You can't protect her forever, y'know."

"I said shut the fuck up." Warren's voice was louder this time.

"You ever give her a bath and"—the man shifted his head, as though looking in Warren's eyes through the rearview mirror—"maybe the thought comes into your head? No, not yet. She's still a couple years too young for that."

Warren jerked the steering wheel and slammed the brakes, stopping the car abruptly. He leapt out, disappearing from view, then appeared at the back door. Swinging it open, he grabbed the man by the hair and smashed his face into the grate that separated the back seats from the front. Then he slammed the door.

His nose bloody, the man stuck out his tongue and groaned, licking the blood.

Cole flipped over his phone. "I can't watch any more."

"You can't see it in the video, but he'd been masturbating through his pants, handcuffs and all, to a picture of *my* little girl. It was too much for me. I knew if I didn't get my emotions under control, I was gonna flip his off switch. Told myself, 'Deep breaths, Rob, deep breaths. Turn around and get back in the front seat.' Took every bit of willpower I had, but I managed to get him to the station without another scratch."

They sat in silence, watching the cars splash by outside.

"I shouldn't have done it," Warren said finally.

"I understand why you did. I feel sick."

"Did he deserve it? Absolutely. Deserves to die, and a lot worse. If you'd seen his apartment, seen the girl." He doubled over, shaking his head like he was trying to erase the memory. "Hell was built for guys like him. And I believe he'll burn there for eternity. But I shouldn't have done what I did."

Cole said nothing. There was nothing to say.

"Now you know," Warren continued. "But you can't write this. I can't give you a copy, and no one can know I showed it to you. I have to let it play out."

Cole thought for a moment, then said, "As disgusted as I am by that video, seeing the context of what you did reminds me of a C.S. Lewis quote. I can't remember the exact phrasing, but it has to do with enemies. When you hear about some atrocity committed by your enemy, you get angry, right? But what if you then learn that the atrocity wasn't nearly as bad as you'd heard at first? If you pay attention to your reaction at that moment, you can learn a lot about yourself."

"I don't get it."

"In that moment, after you learn that your enemy isn't as bad as you thought, are you disappointed because you can't be as mad, or are you relieved on behalf of humanity because your enemy isn't as bad as you feared?"

"I don't know."

"I didn't either, until right now. A week ago I probably would have been disappointed to learn the context. Now, I feel relieved. I wanted to believe the worst of you—another abusive cop in a system that creates them, which is why I didn't work harder to get the full story. Now I'm relieved to learn the context, and it leads me to something else. I *have* to write this. My boss told me something the other day—he drives me crazy but he's usually right—told me sometimes the facts are different than the truth. I can write it in such a way that it never gets back to you."

"No."

"I don't have to mention the video. I'll call the department and—"

"What? What would you do?"

Cole thought. "I'd give it to another reporter at *The Sun*, so I'm not near it. I'll have *them* call the department, we'll find a way to fill out the context."

"The woman who sent me this video wanted me to know it was circulating within the department. But she wasn't supposed to send it. Would get fired for sending it. Plus, you promised."

"I did."

"And you'll keep the promise. Keep your eye on the door. I gotta take a leak."

Warren disappeared into the restroom. Cole stood to get another shot. As she turned toward the bar, movement across the street caught her eye.

The red door opened. An old man limped out.

SHE FROZE. It was him. Michael Wragg. She recognized his limp from the video Mazzalano had shown her. His croaky voice still lived inside her.

She shot a look toward the bathrooms.

"Ma'am, can I help you?" the bartender asked.

"Tell my friend I went across the street. I'll come back to pay…"

She ran out and ducked behind a van. She'd left her jacket behind, so the freezing rain soaked through her shirt as Wragg limped down the street and into Trân's Fried Fish. A minute later, he exited and walked back to the red door. Stopping under the awning, he pressed his face into the white plastic bag and inhaled.

She glanced into the bar. Warren was still in the bathroom.

Casually, she strolled across the street as Wragg opened the door and entered. He disappeared up the stairwell as the door closed slowly on its hinge. Cole jogged the last few paces, then lunged with her right foot, sticking it in the crack before the door closed. She listened as Wragg ascended the concrete steps.

She had two options. Follow Wragg up the stairs, or wait for Warren to come looking for her, then confront Wragg together. But Warren might convince her to call the police, and her journalistic instincts had kicked in. She wanted to be first to the story. That wasn't the only reason she was tempted to follow him up. Wragg's email was seared into her mind. He knew something about Matt.

She rubbed the spot on her lower back where he'd pressed the knife. There was a Band-Aid over it now, and it stung. As she pressed into it, the rage rose in her chest. The static followed the rage, overwhelming it but leaving the urge to pursue the man who'd used her grief against her.

She stepped forward, but something stopped her. Warren's voice in her head, telling her to take a beat. She had to wait for him.

"Yes," Warren said. "W-R-A-G-G. You got the address?… Yes…Yes…Thank you."

He ended the call and stepped out of the restroom. Cole was no longer at the table.

He ran to the counter. "Where'd she go?"

"Across the street. Didn't pay, either. Can you please—"

Warren sprinted for the exit and saw Cole standing in the doorway of Wragg's building. She waved him over.

"He came out," she whispered, glancing up the stairwell. "Then went back upstairs. Let's go."

She turned to head into the building, but Warren

grabbed her shoulder. "Wait a sec. Where did he go when he left?"

"Fish place on the corner."

Warren looked down the block, then stepped back from the building and looked up, taking in the size and layout. "Wait here." He jogged down the block, peered into Trần's Fried Fish, and stopped at the alley just past the restaurant.

An old metal fire escape led up to the third floor. Wragg's apartment.

Returning to Cole, he said, "Fire escape. I'll climb it, you creep up to the door and wait until you hear me."

She nodded apprehensively.

Warren put a hand on her shoulder. "You'll wait until you hear me, right?"

"Got it."

She disappeared into the building as Warren jogged back to the alley. He stopped below the retractable ladder, designed to bridge the gap between the alley and the first landing of the fire escape. But the ladder would let out a screech if he pulled it down. He shot a look up and down the alley, then leapt and grabbed a metal slat on the landing. Like a pole dancer, he kicked his legs up over his head and used his arms to push himself up and over the railing.

As he landed on the grated metal landing, his prosthetic foot slipped between a crack. He tugged at it angrily, but it caught between the slats, pulling the socket loose from the spot where it connected to his knee. The prosthetic fell onto the landing with a loud clang.

Back pressed into the wall, Cole ascended the first twelve

steps, stopping on the second floor landing. She peered up toward Wragg's door. Everything was silent.

Slowly, she climbed the remaining flight of stairs, stopping in front of Wragg's door, listening for Warren between her steady, quiet breaths.

In the apartment, Wragg heard footsteps in the hallway. He dropped the bag of fish on the desk and pulled a silenced .22 from the drawer. He was probably about to be arrested, or killed, but he'd take out one or two of them on his way out.

At the door, he looked through the peephole, expecting to see a team of men in suits or tactical gear. He smiled when he saw Jane Cole, the pretty, blue-eyed reporter with straight black hair.

The .22 in his right hand, he swung open the door with his left, grabbed her by the hair, and yanked her into his apartment.

Warren crouched to pick up his prosthetic. Luckily, the upper portion was too wide to fit through the slots. Sweat beading on his forehead, he looked up. His left leg was strong enough to hop up the two remaining stories, but what if he had to fight? He *had* to reattach it.

Sitting, he smoothed the cloth sheath that he wore like a large sock over his knee and began to attach the leg.

29

COLE HELD her breath in the corner.

A dog lay beside her, breathing weakly. He appeared to be at death's door.

"Did you ring the bell half an hour ago?" Wragg's voice was unmistakably that of the man from last night.

She let out a long, slow breath, trying to calm herself. "Yes. I'm not armed."

"Are you alone?"

"Yes. I'm not police, I think you know. Just a reporter."

"Why did you come here?"

"I wanted to ask you some questions, that's all." Warren would be looking for her. She needed to stay alive as long as she could. She needed to keep him talking, but couldn't think of a good lie. "You were paid by Chandler Price, correct?"

Wragg spat at her. A thick wad of green phlegm landed between her and the dog. "Paid? You make it sound like I'm a hired killer. I'm a freedom fighter. Chandler, too. He's one of our benefactors."

"Benefactors to do what? What is this about?"

Something dinged in the corner and Cole followed the sound to Wragg's desk. A computer with a large monitor. Gun still on Cole, he backed up slowly. His eyes darted to the screen, then back to Cole. "You'll know soon enough."

Cole let the room fall away. She had tunnel vision for Wragg. His gray-blond hair was tied back in a ponytail, his scarred face pinched and anxious. "Where are the other eight rifles?"

He flinched. "You know about those?"

His computer dinged again. His eyes moved back and forth from the screen to Cole.

"We know everything," Cole said.

"We?"

"Me and...my colleagues. If you kill me, everything comes out." Cole tried to convey confidence, to fake self-assuredness. "You think I'd come here without a plan? If they don't hear from me within an hour..."

Wragg swiveled his office chair and sat, gun still on Cole. "You're lying."

Something important was happening on the screen. Something he wanted to read. It pulled his attention toward it and away from her. Wragg still trained the gun on her, and he could fire at any moment, but his mind was on the screen.

"What's your dog's name?"

"Jefferson." He looked back and forth between her and the screen. "I should have named him Hamilton." He laughed. "Because he's weak."

"How did you know about Monkey Tree? And Matty?"

He glanced at her, a strange smile on his face, but said nothing.

Cole saw movement at the window. A hand. She

looked at Wragg. "Are you chatting with whoever has the other eight weapons?"

He stood, smiling broadly. His crooked yellow teeth filled her view. "You know much less than you think." He aimed the gun at her chest. "A moment ago I told you you'd understand everything soon enough. You won't."

A loud scraping came from the window. Jefferson perked up suddenly and yelped. Cole followed the dog's head as it turned.

Warren's feet swung through the window into the apartment. His torso followed.

Wragg spun around and aimed the .22. "Jefferson, sic him!"

The dog leapt up, but lunged toward Wragg as the old man fired wildly.

30

WARREN HEARD two shots as he swung his head into the apartment. The first missed entirely and the second struck his prosthetic leg and ricocheted into the wall. Cole was in the corner, Wragg standing by his computer, a black and white dog nipping at his heels.

Leaping to his feet, Warren lowered his shoulder and bolted toward Wragg. He launched himself over the dog, striking Wragg in the chest before he could get off another shot. They toppled over the chair, Wragg slamming the corner of the desk and falling to the floor. Warren landed beside him.

The computer crashed to the floor. Fried fish erupted from a container, splattering the screen. The baseball bat display case slid off the desk and shattered on the floor. The bat rolled across the wooden floor and stopped at Cole's feet.

Fumbling with his grip on the gun, Wragg rolled toward the window.

Cole grabbed the bat and jumped up.

Warren dove onto Wragg and slammed his wrist back, jarring the gun loose.

Cole kicked it across the room.

A hand on each wrist, Warren pressed Wragg into the floor. Half his size, the old man had no chance of escape. He wasn't even trying.

Cole followed Wragg's gaze to the computer screen, still lit up but speckled with grease and tiny bits of garlic and green onion.

She saw it in his eyes. For the first time, the old man looked afraid.

Thinking quickly, Cole stowed the bat in the crook of her arm and pulled her cell phone from her pocket. Crouching next to the computer, she took a photo of the screen. She wiped away some of the food. Adrenaline coursed through her body and her hand shook as she snapped more photos.

Jefferson had grabbed a fish carcass and was devouring it in the corner.

Still pinned, Wragg said, "You stupid bastard." He spat in Warren's face. "Aren't you that cop who broke that guy's face? You gonna break mine?"

In one deft move, Warren spun him onto his stomach. "Throw me that tape."

Cole tossed him a roll of silver duct tape that had spilled out of a desk drawer. Warren bound Wragg's wrists, then sat him up and stood over him. Cole stood next to him.

Wragg frowned at them contemptuously. "A lying journalist and a disgraced cop."

Cole gripped the bat tight. "Shut up."

Wragg looked at Warren. "She let you into her yet?" Then to Cole. "Monkey Tree, please tell me you're not banging this guy? What would your dear dead Matty think?"

Warren glared down at him. "Shut the hell up, old man."

Through the static, the rage moved inside Cole. Wragg's head was at the perfect level. Waist high.

"Monkey Tree," Wragg said, "I have a confession to make. I don't actually know what happened to Matty. But I do know one thing. When there's so little information about a military death, it usually means friendly fire. Or a cover-up. You know why we're in Afghanistan, right? Your husband was a servant to bankers and globalists. Oil monarchs and the CIA. Not his fault. He probably didn't know any better. Or maybe he does know better and he went AWOL. Hell, maybe he found himself a nice Afghan wife. Monkey Tree 2.0?"

Cole imagined swinging the bat. She felt strong enough to knock his head off clean with a single swing.

"I'm not saying he was sacrificed, but if you don't believe the people in charge would do it, you're naive. Hell, maybe he killed himself to get away from his bitch journalist wife."

She jerked the bat back, ready to strike.

"Jane!" Warren's voice cut through the static. "Jane." His hand was on her shoulder, pulling her back gently. "Jane, you can't."

She let out a long breath and tears filled her eyes.

Warren took the bat.

There was a sudden movement on the floor. Wragg had

lunged down and kicked a leg toward the computer. Warren dropped on top of him.

Wragg's front door swung open and Cole looked up.

Two officers stood in the doorway. "Nobody move!" one of them yelled.

Cole put her hands up.

Warren held Wragg on the ground, his back to the door.

"Up. Get off him," the officer yelled.

"Sir, I am Robert Warren, NYPD sixth precinct. Currently on paid leave. His weapon is there." He nodded at Wragg's .22, a yard away on the floor.

"Stand slowly, hands up."

Warren stood slowly, hands on his head, then stepped aside. As he did, Wragg kicked the computer screen violently. Once. Twice. A third time.

"Don't move!" the officer shouted.

He kicked again, cracking it. Rolling over, he yanked at the cord, pulling it from the wall, then collapsed on the floor, panting.

"Don't move again. We *will* shoot you."

Wragg was still.

"Stand slowly, with your hands up."

Wragg obeyed.

"Turn around."

He turned toward them, a grin across his face. "An international brotherhood, united by General Ki to carry out a singular mission: to bring an end to the great replacement, to restore the sovereignty of nations, to birth a new era of freedom."

He took a tiny step back, then another, inching toward the window. In an instant, Cole knew what he was going to do.

"Don't move!" the officer shouted.

Another step. "I'm free." He said it quietly, as though to himself.

"Do. Not. Move."

Wragg spun on his heels and dove through the open window, crashing onto the fire escape. He stood, wobbling, as one of the officers reached the window and swiped at his leg. Before he could reach him, Wragg threw himself over the metal railing of the fire escape.

After a second, Cole heard the meaty *thwack* of his body hitting the pavement three stories below.

31

Wednesday

COLE STUDIED her boss's eyes. She'd never before been able to read Max Herr, but she could now. His hands were folded neatly in his lap. He hadn't stroked his beard once this morning. She didn't know why he was lying, only that he was.

"You had the Warren story right from the beginning," he said. "We're not running a retraction."

"I had the facts right, but I was missing context. I can't write about the new information I have. But a simple retraction saying something like, 'We may have published with incomplete information and the public deserves to see the outcome of the official inquiry.' Easy."

"I talked to a couple sources in the department and they wouldn't give me any details. They assured me that Warren is a bad apple. A brutal cop. Then I don't hear from you for two days and you want to run a retraction based on a video you claim to have seen? Jane, no."

"Max, c'mon, have the decency not to lie to my face.

What the hell is going on? First you ask me to continue looking into it, then I do and now you're stonewalling me?"

He stood, flummoxed, then sat back down. "Fine," he sighed, his demeanor changing suddenly. "But it doesn't leave this room, okay?"

She nodded.

"Local community groups want blood on this, and the police department is gonna give it to them. They're gonna dump Warren around Christmas when no one is looking. We don't need to run a retraction. You said it yourself. Nothing in your story was wrong."

It hit her like a kick to the stomach. She stood, fists clenched. "They're gonna fire him? What about the union, the trial, or whatever?"

He shook his head.

"If we raise hell," she continued passionately, "we could save him. I'm telling you, there is context the public needs to know."

"It's over, Cole. His career is over."

"What are we doing here if we're not willing to fight on this?"

Max leaned back in his chair. "Living to fight another day."

There was a long silence, then her boss said, "We need to talk about what happened yesterday. I know you're not going to write about yourself, but you understand we have to report on it. Susan will want to interview you about what happened inside Wragg's apartment."

Cole frowned. "Hope she enjoys hearing, 'No comment.'"

She'd spent the evening with the police, explaining how she'd come to be in Michael Wragg's apartment. In a brief exchange with Warren before they'd been driven in separate cars to the police station, she'd convinced him to lie. "Tell them you heard screaming and climbed the fire escape. Tell them we've never met. I didn't break any laws and I don't have to give up my sources. I'll take all the heat."

And that's exactly what she'd done. She'd gotten the interview with Margaret Price, which had tipped her off to Chandler Price. An anonymous tip had connected Price to Wragg and she'd ended up in his apartment. Nope, she'd never met Robert Warren, but she was lucky he happened to be at the fish restaurant when she started screaming. That's what she'd told the police.

She'd called Max Herr from the station, telling him what happened and suggesting that he assign another reporter to follow up on the story. No official statement had been issued by the police connecting Wragg to the murder of Raj Ambani, but it would drop soon.

"Max, please, I can't walk out of here without trying one last time. Run a retraction on my Robert Warren story."

"No."

She thought for a minute, then said something she'd never imagined saying. "Then I quit."

She waited for him to speak, but he said nothing. Without another word, she turned and walked out.

32

COLE COMPOSED her text to Danny Aravilla at the bar across the street from Wragg's apartment. Outside, TV crews were filming and a few print reporters hung around, trying to get information from local residents.

Cole: *I think we both know this isn't working. You're a great guy, but I'm not ready for anything real. I thought maybe I could be, but you probably know better than anyone that I'm not. Let's call it quits before you start hating me.*

Breaking up with someone via text was terrible. She'd spent two days trying to convince herself to do it in person, but the thought of his hand on the redhead's hips made her fear the confrontation. She wasn't sure if she was more worried for herself, or for him.

She sent the text as Warren arrived and handed the bartender a credit card. "Coffee for me." Warren pointed at the bar in front of Cole. "Patrón, neat, for her. And leave it open. Oh yeah—add on whatever we owe for yesterday."

Bruce Springsteen's version of *Santa Claus Is Comin' to Town* filled the air as they stared at the muted TVs above the bar.

Cole dreaded telling him what her boss had said, but she owed it to him to break the news in person. "There's something I need to tell you."

"You gonna tell me that I'm getting fired?"

"What? How'd you know?"

The bartender set down their drinks and Cole gestured to the tequila. "You sure you want to pay for this? You're contributing to my consumption of empty carbs."

"Gotta look on the bright side." Warren winked and took a long sip of his coffee. "At least it's not a margarita."

"The coffee sufficiently burnt?" Cole asked.

"Could have used an extra hour on the burner, but it'll do." He sighed before getting back to the subject. "My old training officer Gabriela called this morning. She got wind of it."

"How do they justify that? I mean, I thought the police were supposed to protect their own and all that. That attitude used to infuriate me. Y'know, as a reporter."

"Usually do." He shook his head. "The relationship between the NYPD and the city is always on edge. Don't ever print this, but I think it almost makes the department feel good to get rid of a black cop for brutality. They get enough bad press with the shit white cops do. Now they can say, 'Hey look, black cops rough up suspects, too.'"

"That's sick." Cole shot her tequila. "So how'd you know that's what I was going to say?"

"You looked like you were going to tell me my puppy died."

"Speaking of puppies, what happens to the dog? Jefferson."

"If there aren't any relatives who'll take him, and I'm guessing there aren't, protocol is to take him to the shelter. But I know a retired cop who takes care of animals found at crime scenes. Nurtures them back to health and personally finds homes for each and every one. Already got a call in to him about Jefferson."

Cole smiled, relieved. "I'm glad he'll be cared for." She looked around the bar. "You know, I like this place. Not a cop bar, not a journalist bar."

"Speaking of that, I want to apologize, for, uh, maligning your sacred profession and all that. You were just doing your job."

"No, *I* should be apologizing to *you*. Threatening to call your wife and drag up all your issues in the past. The incident was newsworthy. The other stuff wasn't. I never would have written about it out of spite. Empty threat, and I shouldn't have said it."

"We were both upset. Now, we're square."

They sat in silence, staring up at the flat screen TV. When CNN returned from commercials, a segment about Raj Ambani started. "They still have nothing," Cole said. "It'll take them another day to connect Wragg to Ambani."

"You think he acted alone?"

"Of course not. He practically confessed to an international conspiracy. I told the officers who interviewed me what he said. They wrote it down, but kinda shrugged it off. What did you make of what he said?"

"Barely followed it."

Cole closed her eyes and let the memory fill the void. "An international brotherhood, united by General Ki to carry out a singular mission: to bring an end to the great replacement, to restore the sovereignty of nations, to birth a new era of freedom."

"What the hell does that mean? Sounds like some bullshit Nazi propaganda."

"I don't know. I googled it and nothing came up with

that exact phrase. Best I can tell, it's a part of an ideology that exists in many countries. Ultra-nationalist, anti-globalization, anti-immigration, pro-sovereignty. Sometimes tinged with racism and patriarchy, sometimes not."

"Yeah. Like I said, Nazi bullshit."

"It includes some, but there are a lot of other strains of thought mixed in. It often gets dismissed as far-right extremism, but it's...I don't know. The way he said it chilled me."

"That reminds me," Warren said. "In the apartment, you took photos of his screen. Why'd you do that, and what were they?"

"While he had me in there, he was looking at his screen, something was going down. When it fell to the ground, I don't know, I thought, 'What if it turns off and the data isn't recoverable?' I did what people do now, take pictures and look at them later."

"So, did you? Did you look at them?"

She pulled out her phone. "Only got a few. Screen was covered with food at first. I got one clear image, but it didn't make any sense." She slid the phone to Warren, open to the picture.

It was a crooked image of Wragg's screen with flecks of food and smears of sauce, but a small amount of text was legible in the center.

Kokutai-Goji:

2/9

(The Silver Squirrel)

Final Notice.

An international brotherhood, united by General Ki to carry out a singular mission: to bring an end to the great replacement, to restore the sovereignty of nations, to birth a new era of freedom.

2/9

Final Notice.

When he'd finished reading, Warren said, "You need to show this to the police."

"Forwarded it to them. Plus financial records from Chandler Price. I gave them everything except you. Far as they know, you had nothing to do with anything."

"You know, the First Amendment doesn't protect you on those documents. You can't go to jail for writing about them, but if a judge orders you to tell him where you got them, you'll have to."

"There are shield laws, and I doubt it'll come to that. It's weird, I feel like I've heard the phrase 'Silver Squirrel' before. Ring any bells for you?"

"I got nothing." Warren paid the tab and slid his stool back from the bar. "I gotta get home. Get a workout in and get some rest. I'm seeing my daughter tomorrow."

Cole smiled. "That'll be nice. I'll see you around."

"See you around." He headed for the door.

Cole let her eyes land on the TV above the bar. "Wait!"

CNN had a *Breaking News* banner on the screen. The bartender was fumbling with the remote. The bar grew quiet as every eye fixed on the screen. Warren stood behind Cole as the bartender turned on the sound.

"In shocking news tonight," a male news anchor said gravely, "former Vice President Alvin Meyers has died in what appears to be an assassination-style murder in Washington, D.C. Born and raised in Virginia, Meyers served as a US Senator from 1970 to 1992, and Governor of Virginia from 1992 to 2000. He then accepted the role of Vice President. Details are still coming in. Sources tell CNN there are no known political motivations at this time. Since his retirement in 2008, Meyers sat on the boards of some of the nation's top companies, and became an international ambassador for American business. Stay with us this evening as we bring in expert guests and former colleagues to mourn his death and speak about his legacy."

"It's connected," Cole said.

Warren sat. "Maybe, but possibly not."

"It's connected. I know for sure."

"How can you know that? We don't know if it was one of the other guns. Maybe you know of some connection between Ambani and Meyers, but I don't. Why do you look like that? Jane, what's going on?"

"The name Silver Squirrel. I remember why it sounded familiar. It was his Secret Service code name when he was VP." She handed her phone to Warren. Together, they reread the message from the picture of Wragg's screen.

"Two-slash-nine," Warren said. "That could mean two *out of* nine. Nine rifles. Raj Ambani was number one. Meyers is number two." He ran a hand over his head, letting out a long sigh. "I don't even want to think about what this means."

"I *know* what it means." Cole steadied her eyes on his. "It means this is just beginning."

--End--

PREVIEW OF THE CRIME BEAT, EPISODE 2: WASHINGTON, D.C.

Wednesday

THROUGH THE DIN of punk music that filled the crowded bar, Jane Cole struggled to hear the TV news anchor stumble over the breaking news.

"Former Vice President Alvin Meyers has been murdered...we're hearing...I've just been told..."

She waved down the bartender. "Can you turn up the television?"

A man rushed from a nearby table and slid onto the stool next to her. He pointed at the screen. "Holy hell! Meyers got shot. Turn it up!"

The bartender turned off the music and the sudden quiet drew more attention. Dozens of eyes locked on the TV above the bar. As the bartender turned up the volume, Cole relaxed, no longer needing to fight so hard to pick up the anchor's words.

The newscaster brought his finger to his ear. "I'm hearing that...my apologies...all we can confirm at this time is that former Vice President Alvin Meyers has been killed.

After this quick break, we'll be back with more on this stunning news story."

Next to Cole, Robert Warren sipped his coffee, eyes on the TV. She faced him. "Right now, every news producer in the world is trying to decide whether to air videos of a former Vice President being murdered. That poor anchor has a half dozen people arguing in his ear."

"He's doing a decent job, given the circumstances."

She dropped her eyes to her phone. The shooting wasn't trending on Twitter yet, but it would be soon. Her feed was cluttered with various versions of "OMG, Alvin Meyers is dead," and "Who bothers to assassinate an ex-VP?" One Tweet stood out—a wobbly cellphone video claiming to show the moments just before he died.

Posted by someone at the event, the video showed the crowded rooftop of The Watergate. On the left, two bartenders in black and white poured wine behind a curved wooden bar. Waiters shifted in and out of the shot, setting glasses on trays, then disappearing from the frame. Between the bar and the railings that separated the rooftop from the sky, forty to fifty people chatted in small groups, sipping drinks. Some stood by the railings, staring in the direction of the apartment buildings and hotels that loomed across the Potomac.

"Looks like a typical D.C. cocktail party," Cole said.

"You know what it was for?"

"I saw something on the scroll about a fundraiser for a world literacy program. Something like that. Alvin Meyers was one of the more *involved* former vice presidents. Boards of directors, international foundations, that kind of stuff."

"Why didn't he run for president?"

Cole shot him a look. "Really?"

"What? I don't follow politics."

"There are a few videos of him being a little handsy with female interns. Nothing *too* bad, but enough to get him burned alive by the Democratic base."

"I thought getting handsy was a requirement for being president these days," Warren said.

"Meyers made millions as a private citizen. That could also be why he didn't run."

Cole held the phone between them as the Twitter video made a quick, disorienting pan to the right, as though the person holding the phone had been bumped or turned quickly. The shot was now centered on a glass door where Alvin Meyers entered, flanked by two men in black suits. The one on the left muttered into the sleeve of his jacket. Secret Service.

Meyers was blandly handsome. Tall, with silver-white hair and a constant smile that was probably necessary in his line of work but struck her as phony.

For the next thirty seconds, the video followed Meyers as he shook hands, slapped backs, and repeated different versions of the catch phrase he'd used for years: "What's good for the world is good for America."

Then, in an instant, Meyers' hand shot to his neck, like he'd been stung by an invisible hornet. He dropped out of the frame. People screamed. A Secret Service agent pointed at the railing. The other agent crouched, also disappearing from the frame. The video jerked and showed only a blur of backs and flailing arms. A shriek pierced the scene.

A woman shouted, "Meyers is down!"

"It came from over there," a man called.

The video jerked again, a shot of heads and sky, then ended.

Cole scrolled for a few seconds, looking for information

or other videos, then glanced at Warren. "No footage of Meyers after he was hit. And no footage of where the shot came from. At least not yet."

"Right away, Secret Service would have had Meyers in the elevator, then in the back of his armored vehicle, racing away from the scene. Protocol, even if they knew he was dead." Warren pressed his hands to his cheeks and let out a long breath of air. His pressure-release valve. "If he was the President, they'd have had bags of his blood in the limo. Not that it matters if the shot was on target."

Warren nodded at the TV. The broadcast was back from commercial and the anchor had recovered his composure. "Initial reports from the scene—and please keep in mind that these are *unconfirmed* reports—but initial reports from the scene indicate that the shot may not have come from someone on the rooftop. Perhaps a neighboring building, we're being told." The anchor paused, focusing on the voice of the producer in his ear. "For those just joining us, in breaking news, former Vice President Alvin Meyers was shot and killed this evening, and we will be here all night with special coverage of his death, and his legacy. Stay with us."

"First thing that pops to mind," Cole said. "How does Alvin Meyers connect to Raj Ambani?"

"I don't know much about him."

"Moderate Democrat. Four-term Senator, two-term Governor of Virginia before being picked for VP."

"And he cashed in when he left office?"

"Yup. Hundred-fifty grand per speech, seven-figure book deal, the works."

"So he's well off and powerful, two things he had in common with Ambani. But what do they have to do with each other?"

Cole did a quick search on her phone. She clicked the first link. "I thought so," she said, holding it up to Warren. "Ambani hosted a fundraiser for Meyers, and has donated money to him."

Warren was skeptical. "Don't businessmen like Ambani donate to all the candidates, Republican and Democrat, just to make sure?"

"We need to start somewhere, and that's a connection."

Warren gave a short nod. "Why not start in D.C.?"

She stared at him blankly.

"I have a car."

His meaning hit her suddenly. "You serious, Rob?"

He nodded.

Cole scrolled through Twitter as she considered. She'd quit her job on a whim less than six hours ago. She hadn't given it much thought, but now she was hoping for some freelance work to tide her over while she looked for something permanent. And if the Meyers killing *was* connected to the Ambani murder, this was about to become the biggest story in the world.

She was about to ask Warren what kind of car he had when a text arrived from Joey Mazzalano—a scumbag Lieutenant from the fifth precinct, but also one of her best sources.

The Italian Stallion: *Buy me a drink tonight. Antonio's at 10.*

She considered ignoring him, but tapped out a quick reply.

Jane Cole: *Why?*

The Italian Stallion: *You said you always pay your debts, and that Wragg tip was shit.*

Jane Cole: *The Wragg tip was spot on.*

The Italian Stallion: *He died before I could get any credit,* *and you could have called me when you found the apartment. Plus, I have something for you.*

Cole let out an exasperated sigh and went back to Twitter. Her eye landed on another video from the roof of The Watergate, which showed a different angle on the scene. She held it up for Warren to watch with her.

While the video played, she considered Warren's offer again. Until recently, she'd believed he was an abusive cop who should be fired and prosecuted. The dashcam footage had shown that he'd been provoked in the worst way possible. She didn't think she would have been able to keep her cool if a pedophile rapist had made that kind of comment in her presence. But still, she felt uneasy about hopping in his car for the four-hour drive to D.C.

The new video didn't have a clear shot of Meyers. Just people drinking casually before the shooting, and screaming in panic afterwards. When it ended, Warren plucked the phone from her hand and laid it face down on the bar. He waited until she met his dark eyes.

"Cole," he said. "Right now, I've got nothing else in my life. Nothing but this case."

"You don't *have* this case. You're not a cop anymore."

"In America you need a special license to drive a taxi, need to pass the bar exam to practice law. Hell, you need a permit to serve hot dogs at the fair. Cops have to pass mental and physical tests, written exams. But you don't need anything except a laptop to be a journalist."

She didn't know what he was driving at, but she wasn't up for another fight about cops and journalists. "It's called the First Amendment."

"That's what I'm saying. I want to get to the bottom of this. I bet you do, too. We can sit here all night watching the news and looking at blurry clips online, and my guess is there will be more and more blurry clips like this. But you and I are the only two people alive who know about the guns, about Chandler Price, and the screenshots. If Meyers is connected, we have a better chance of figuring out how than anyone. Let's go to D.C. and do what we both do best."

His face was pleading, earnest. She recognized that look. It was the one thing they had in common—that indefinable, relentless need to learn the truth. If they could, it would be the biggest story of her life. She nodded at the bartender. "Can we settle up, please?"

"So we're going?"

"We're going, but I need to make a quick stop on the way out of town. Gotta meet a source."

"Who?"

Cole exhaled sharply and pressed her hand across her forehead.

"You okay?" Warren asked.

Cole sent a quick text, agreeing to meet with Mazzalano, then said, "Pick me up outside Antonio's in Little Italy in an hour."

End Sample. Episode 2 Now Available.

AUTHOR NOTES, AUGUST 2019

Thanks for reading!

It's been nine months since my last book came out, but it has felt like an eternity. Folks in my Facebook group have been hounding me for a new series, and I'm thrilled *The Crime Beat* is finally here.

I'm working with a consultant on this series, a man named Gary Collins. I met Gary at the 20Books Writing Conference in November of 2018, and we hit it off right away. For *The Crime Beat*, Gary is providing important insights into weaponry, military life, and police work. He's also a consistent sounding board and story fixer. Many of the coolest little nuggets in this series were his idea. In addition to having a military and law enforcement background I don't have, Gary is the author of seven non-fiction books. Find out more about them, and about Gary, by flipping a few pages.

Now, some thanks…

Special thanks to everyone in the A.C. Fuller Fiction Fans Group on Facebook. Your interest in my work—plus your constant support and encouragement—keeps me going.

Thanks to the good people at Rocking Book Covers, who designed the art for all the books in *The Crime Beat* series.

Thanks to Chet Sandberg, who edited this book, to Noah Brand, who also edited it, and to Jennifer Karchmer, who proofread it. And to Kay Vreeland, who caught some errors at the last second before publication.

Thanks to my wife Amanda, who read multiple versions of this book and improved it in so many ways. And to my children, Arden and Charlie, for giving me time to write it.

Thanks to Rebecca Scherer at the Jane Rotrosen Agency, whose valuable feedback made this book much better.

And to the readers who enjoy my books, thank you so much!

Over the next few months, *The Crime Beat* will be taking me all around the world. I hope you'll come along for the ride!

A.C. Fuller

ABOUT THE AUTHOR

Once a journalist in New York, A.C. Fuller now writes stories at the intersection of media, politics, and technology. He also teaches writing workshops around the country and internationally.

Before he began writing full time, he was an adjunct professor of journalism at NYU and an English teacher at Northwest Indian College.

He now lives with his wife, two children, and two dogs near Seattle. For a free copy of one of A.C.'s books, check out: www.acfuller.com / readerclub.

You can find out more at www.acfuller.com

OTHER BOOKS BY A.C. FULLER

THE ALEX VANE MEDIA THRILLERS

Follow journalist Alex Vane from 9/11 into the social media age in the breakout thriller series from A.C. Fuller.

The Cutline
(An Alex Vane Prequel Novella)—Available *free*, and only though my website
The Anonymous Source
(An Alex Vane Media Thriller, Book 1)
The Inverted Pyramid
(An Alex Vane Media Thriller, Book 2)
The Mockingbird Drive
(An Alex Vane Media Thriller, Book 3)
The Shadow File
(An Alex Vane Media Thriller, Book 4)
The Last Journalist
(An Alex Vane Media Thriller, Book 5)

AMERITOCRACY

The two-party system was broken, so Mia Rhodes created an alternative. Welcome to Ameritocracy, the new political series readers are calling "The West Wing meets Survivor" and "Mr. Smith Goes to Washington for the social media age."

Open Primary
(Ameritocracy, Book 1)
Off Message
(Ameritocracy, Book 2)
Echo Chamber
(Ameritocracy, Book 3)

PRAISE FOR A.C. FULLER'S BOOKS:

"A talented new writer sure to do damage to the best-seller lists."
-Robert Dugoni, #1 Amazon and New York Times
Bestselling Author of *My Sister's Grave*

"Elite Indie Reads anticipates that Fuller will soon be a household name."
-Elite Indie Reads

"An ode to American news served just the way I like it--fast, bloody, and utterly righteous."
-Roger Hobbs, New York Times Bestselling Author of Ghostman

ABOUT GARY COLLINS, CONSULTANT ON THE CRIME BEAT

Gary Collins has a unique background that includes military intelligence, Special Agent for the U.S. State Department Diplomatic Security Service, U.S. Department of Health and Human Services, and U.S. Food and Drug Administration. Gary's background and expertise bring a much-needed perspective to the topics of simple living, health, nutrition, entrepreneurship, self-help and self-reliance. He holds an AS degree in Exercise Science, a BS in Criminal Justice, and an MS in Forensic Science.

His website, www.thesimplelifenow.com, and *The Simple Life* book series (his total lifestyle reboot), blow the lid off of conventional life and wellness expectations, and are essential for every person seeking a simpler and happier life.

You can find all his books on Amazon here.

The Simple Life Guide To Financial Freedom: Free Yourself from the Chains of Debt and Find Financial Peace

The Simple Life Guide To Decluttering Your Life: The How-To Book of Doing More With Less and Focusing on the Things That Matter

The Simple Life Guide To RV Living: The Road to Freedom and the Mobile Lifestyle Revolution

The Simple Life Guide To Optimal Health: How to Get Healthy and Feel Better Than Ever

Living Off The Grid: What To Expect While Living the Life of Ultimate Freedom and Tranquility

Going Off The Grid: The How-To Book of Simple Living and Happiness

The Beginner's Guide To Living Off The Grid: The DIY Workbook for Living the Life You Want

Made in the USA
Monee, IL
06 April 2021